Makers

Place

STACEY AND
THE CHEERLEADERS

**Other books by
Ann M. Martin**

Leo the Magnificat
Rachel Parker, Kindergarten Show-off
Eleven Kids, One Summer
Ma and Pa Dracula
Yours Turly, Shirley
Ten Kids, No Pets
Slam Book
Just a Summer Romance
Missing Since Monday
With You and Without You
Me and Katie (the Pest)
Stage Fright
Inside Out
Bummer Summer

THE KIDS IN MS. COLMAN'S CLASS series
BABY-SITTERS LITTLE SISTER series
THE BABY-SITTERS CLUB mysteries
THE BABY-SITTERS CLUB series

STACEY AND THE CHEERLEADERS

Ann M. Martin

AN
APPLE
PAPERBACK

SCHOLASTIC INC.
New York Toronto London Auckland Sydney

Cover art by Hodges Soileau

ISBN 0-590-92601-2

12 11 10 9 8 7 6 5 4 3   2   8 9/9 0 1 2/0

The author gratefully acknowledges
Peter Lerangis
for his help in
preparing this manuscript.

CHAPTER 1

"Watch out!"

The shout startled me. Before I could turn around, something hit my shoulder. It threw me off balance. My books went flying, my feet shot out from under me, and I fell.

I, Stacey McGill, was a victim of the winter's first snowball. Or one of the first, anyway.

Until that moment, it had been a great morning. Snow had fallen overnight, even though it was only early December. I had wolfed down my breakfast, put on my new plum-colored corduroy pants and white down jacket for the first time, and taken a nice, slow walk to school with my friend Claudia. The sun was blazing away, and Stoneybrook had never looked so gorgeous.

Now, I adore snow. But right then, *sitting* in it was not what I'd had in mind.

As Claudia helped me to my feet, I could

see I'd left two plum-colored streaks in the snow. "Ohhhh, look," I said.

"Hmm, I guess you better wash those pants separately," Claud remarked.

I was too annoyed to laugh. "Thanks," I replied, brushing myself off.

A big shadow loomed behind me. "Sorry. I didn't mean to hit you."

I looked up.

And up . . . and up.

My attacker must have been at least six feet tall. I was eye level with his jacket, which had a varsity letter sewn to it — the letters SMS with a basketball across the middle. (SMS, by the way, stands for Stoneybrook Middle School.)

When I reached his face, my anger melted away. I knew who he was. Everyone in SMS did. RJ Blaser was a star of the SMS basketball team.

I should explain something. This winter our school had been swept up by basketball fever. Our team was number one. Totally undefeated. Even I had started going to the games, and I'm no jock. The *Stoneybrook News*, which never writes about SMS, had printed a big article about the team.

To be hit by a snowball from behind was no fun. To be hit by RJ Blaser? Well, that was different. I felt kind of honored. I had noticed RJ around school (who hadn't?), but this was the first time he had ever looked me in the eye.

"That's okay," I squeaked. "It's . . . soft . . ."

He looked confused. "Your shoulder?"

Claudia rolled her eyes. "No, the *snow*."

"It wasn't hard enough to hurt," I quickly added. "Really."

We stared at each other, smiling and saying nothing. Claudia brushed off the back of mv corduroys with sharp, strong swipes.

"Um, my name is RJ," he said.

"I know," I replied without thinking. "I mean, I went to a basketball game last week and they were calling out your name over the loudspeaker a lot."

RJ's face brightened. "Was that the 64–59 over Mercer or the 70–60 over Lawrenceville?"

"The . . . uh . . . Mercer one, I think."

"Yeah. I scored twenty-seven points and collected five fouls."

Huh? I thought he said *fowls*, and I couldn't remember any chickens running around the basketball court. But I said, "Wow," because I could tell I was supposed to be impressed.

"So that's why they were calling my name," RJ added. Then he pointed toward the school

3

and said, "That's Marty Bukowski. You probably heard his name, too. He's the one I was throwing the snowball at."

I looked across the lawn and recognized Marty. He was with Malik Jaffrey and Wayne McConville, two other drop-dead cute basketball stars. With them were four of the most popular girls in the school: Darcy Redmond, Sheila McGregor, Margie Greene, and Penny Weller — all cheerleaders.

"I guess you better stick to *basket*balls, huh?" Claudia piped up.

RJ gave her a blank look. "Say what?"

"You know, instead of *snow*balls?" Claudia glanced at me warily. She must have thought she was intruding on something, because she started backing away. "Just a joke. Uh, I better get going. I have some questions for my home-room teacher. See you later."

"That's okay — " I began, but Claudia was booking.

As she passed RJ's friends, one of them yelled, "Yo, Blaser. It's cold. We're going in."

"Okay," RJ called back. "Later!"

The group started walking toward school. I was a little disappointed. It would have been cool to meet them.

"It is kind of late," RJ said. "Want to walk with me?"

"Sure," I replied.

As we headed in, I didn't feel the wetness at the back of my corduroys at all. I didn't feel much of anything. I wondered if anyone was actually witnessing my walk with RJ Blaser.

"So, you're . . . ?" RJ was asking me a question.

"I'm fine," I answered.

He flashed a big smile. "No, your *name*. You didn't tell me."

"Oh!" I must have turned red, because I could feel my ears heating up. "I'm Stacey McGill."

He nodded and looked earnestly at the ground. For a moment neither of us said anything. Then, as RJ held open the front door of the school for me, he asked, "Did you see *Mall Warriors II* yet — you know, the movie?"

I shook my head. "Uh-uh."

"Good. We can see it Friday night. It's playing in town. Okay?"

"Okay, sure."

Rrrriinnngg! The homeroom bell echoed through the school.

RJ began trotting down the front hall as if it were a basketball court. "My dad can drive us," he called over his shoulder. "I'll get your address later. See you."

" 'Bye!" I called.

Kids were scurrying to their classrooms. I stood rooted to the spot until no one else was in the hall. It took me a moment to realize I hadn't picked up my books from the snowy sidewalk. I'd have to run out and get them, and I'd be late for homeroom.

But you know what? I didn't care.

I was going to go out with RJ Blaser.

Okay, time out. Do I sound hopelessly boy-crazy? I'm not. I mean, I do like boys, but they're not the only things in my life.

I guess I should tell you about myself. My full name is Anastasia Elizabeth McGill, but please don't ever call me that. (My parents are the only ones who do, and just when they're angry.) I'm an only child. I'm thirteen years old and in eighth grade. My family moved to Stoneybrook when I was twelve. Before that we lived in New York City.

Yes, kids do grow up in the Big Apple — and like it. Does that surprise you? It surprised some kids in Stoneybrook when I first moved here. They believed New York had only office buildings and theaters. And some of them had these weird expectations that all New Yorkers should be warped, nasty, or snobby.

No way. New York does have its problems, but I love the city. Plenty of kids live there, and there's so much to see and do it's *impossible* to be bored.

We first moved to Stoneybrook when my dad's company transferred him here. It's a suburb, but to us it felt like the country. I met some really great friends, including Claudia, and I joined the Baby-sitters Club (more about that later). Then came the McGill Family Drama. We moved back to New York when Dad was relocated *again*, and he and Mom started fighting all the time. Soon they were asking me the Big Question: whom did I want to live with after the divorce?

Well, it wasn't as sudden as it sounds. The problems had been growing for awhile. But nothing had prepared me for how much the divorce would hurt. After lots of crying and arguing and talking, I decided to stay with Mom. Even though I'm such a New Yorker, I had grown to love Stoneybrook, too. And I missed my new friends terribly.

So we were off to Connecticut again, but this time there were only two of us. We've been here ever since. Stoneybrook is just a train ride away from Manhattan. I visit Dad pretty often, so I have the best of both worlds.

What else can I tell you about me? Here are some things I like: clothes, movies, kids, and math. (Yes, math. I can't help it. I'm good at it, and I think numbers are fascinating.)

Here are some things I don't like: snobbiness, seeing people barf, and doctors. Not necessarily in that order. I have to see doctors a lot, and I probably will for the rest of my life. You see, I have diabetes. That means my body can't regulate the amount of sugar in my blood. Have you heard of people who get a "sugar rush" if they eat too much candy? Well, multiply that by a hundred, and that's what I could get if I eat even a small amount of sugar. It's not just a rush, either. I could end up in the hospital. To keep my body running normally I have to give myself daily injections of a drug called insulin. It sounds gross, I know, but you get used to it if you have diabetes.

Now that you know I have a life outside of boys, let's move on to the next subject, which is . . . well, boys. Or, the lack of them in my life.

Have you ever heard the song "Lucky in Love"? It was not written about me. If my love life were a bottle, it would be empty. If it were a place, it would be the Sahara Desert. Or Death Valley.

Okay, I'm exaggerating. But not by much. Let's face it, I may not be boy-*crazy*, but I'm boy-*interested*. I mean, it wouldn't take a lot to make me happy. Just a gorgeous, smart, considerate guy who takes my breath away and happens to love me even more than I love him.

Is that asking too much?

One time I did fall in LUV. Head over heels. He was gorgeous, smart, and considerate. One catch: he was also twenty-two and my substitute math teacher. I thought he was in love with me, but he told me (politely) that I was wrong. It was beyond humiliating. I felt about two inches tall.

Yes, I am interested in boys my own age. I've dated a few SMS guys, but nothing has ever clicked. Sometimes I go out with Pete Black or Austin Bentley, but they're just friends. In other words, plenty of LIKE but no LUV.

My one steady boyfriend was Sam Thomas. We lasted a long time, but we kind of drifted apart and agreed to see other people.

As of that snowy Wednesday morning in December, I was still waiting for the other people.

That snowball may have changed everything. At least I hoped so. RJ was cute. Not gorgeous, but nice to look at. He had curly red hair and hazel eyes and broad shoulders.

Through him, I hoped I'd have a chance to meet some of his teammates and cheerleader friends. I didn't know any of them, but I wanted to. They were definitely the coolest and most popular kids at SMS. The guys were

Major Hunks and incredible athletes (not to mention *tall*, which I find very cool). Every single one of the girls was stunning and talented. Plus you would not believe the amazing clothes they wore. I'd been dying to ask some of them where they bought their outfits. Not anyplace I'd ever been (including all the boutiques I'd been to in New York).

So I was in a pretty good mood that day, even though I was late for homeroom. I tried to sneak in quietly, but it didn't work. Sheila McGregor, one of the cheerleaders I'd seen outside, began giggling when she saw my books. I looked down to see they were dripping with melted snow.

Our teacher, Ms. Levine, raised her eyebrows. "Stacey McGill? Late? What a novel concept." (She talks like that.)

I slunk into my seat. "Sorry."

Ms. Levine harrumphed, then continued making her morning announcements. A minute or two later I felt something poke me on the right side of my back. I moved over a little. Sheila sits behind me, and I figured something on her desk had slipped.

Another poke. I began to turn around. I saw Sheila's hand by my elbow, with a note in it. The note was folded neatly into a triangle. I took it, opened it, and read it:

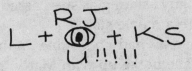

L + <3 + KS
RJ
U !!!!!

P.S. It wasn't an accident. He never misses!

🙂

I couldn't help blushing. Quickly I turned and smiled at Sheila, who smiled back.

Ms. Levine didn't notice. Thank goodness.

After homeroom, Sheila and I walked down the hall together. She gave me this huge grin. "So . . . did he ask you out?"

"Yeah," I replied.

"Lucky," she said. "Maybe you guys and Marty and I can go out together sometime."

"You and Marty?"

She showed me a ring with a jewel in it. "We go steady. Isn't this beautiful?"

It was. I had never, *ever* seen a ring like that on an eighth-grade girl. "Wow."

We said good-bye at the next corner. Sheila's class was in the opposite direction from mine. I watched her for a moment as she walked away. Her hair was so silky and thick, and her clothes showed off her perfect figure. I could see guys staring as she passed them, as if she were a movie star.

Of course *she* had no trouble finding a boyfriend. If she broke up with Marty, she could probably pick from a waiting list.

Must be nice, I thought.

At lunchtime, I sat with my BSC friends. (BSC, by the way, stands for Baby-sitters Club.) We were just yacking away, until I told them about RJ.

You could practically hear their jaws clanking to the ground.

"He asked you *out*?" Kristy Thomas asked the question around a mouthful of Swedish meatball.

"Say it a little louder, Kristy, so *everyone* in the cafeteria can hear," Claudia said.

"Is it so unbelievable?" I asked.

Kristy laughed. "No, I didn't mean it that way. It's just that, you know, the boys in *The Group* always seem to date the girls in *The Group*." (Kristy pronounced "the group" as if it were the title of a movie.)

"Maybe RJ's dated them all already," Claudia remarked.

"You *guys*!" I complained.

"Just kidding!" Claudia shot back.

"I think it's great, Stace," Mary Anne Spier said.

"I admit, he is cute," Kristy conceded.

"Hey, Stacey!" Sheila's voice called out. I looked up and saw her waving to me as she walked into the cafeteria.

"Hi!" I called back.

For a moment I thought she would sit with us. But instead she walked to a table in the back, where The Group was sitting.

I know it sounds weird, but I had an urge to go sit with Sheila. The Group seemed to be having such a great time at their table. Besides, *boys* were there, including RJ.

But the urge went away. Claudia was telling us about a baby-sitting charge who insisted on using a wicker trash basket as a helmet. Soon we were all laughing hysterically, and I forgot about The Group.

You know what? Sheila was not the only cheerleader who was friendly to me that day. Margie Greene, who had never even looked my way, asked me about my outfit in English class. Penny Weller and I had a conversation about makeup in Social Studies.

After school, as I was taking books out of my locker, I saw RJ at the end of the hall. He didn't see me. I hurried up, hoping to run over to him and say hi.

Before I could close the locker, Jessi Ramsey came up from behind me. "Hey, just in time," she said.

Jessi is one of the BSC's two junior members. She's in sixth grade here at SMS. I'd almost forgotten she was meeting me after school that day. She had a sitting job in my neighborhood, so we'd agreed to walk home together.

"Oh, hi, Jessi," I said.

"Ready to go?"

"Yeah, sure."

I closed my locker. As Jessi and I walked to the door, I waved to RJ. He was with a few other Group members. One of them nudged him, and he waved back.

He was grinning.

Guess what. So was I.

CHAPTER 2

"You're *what*?" Kristy blurted into the phone receiver. "You call that 'having a good time'?"

Jessi was fidgeting excitedly. "Let *me* talk to Mal," she pleaded.

Mal is Mallory Pike, the BSC's other junior member. She was getting over a case of mono. Before our Wednesday club meeting officially began, Kristy had decided to call her and find out how she was doing.

"Here's Jessi," Kristy said. "Feel better!"

As Jessi took the receiver, Kristy shook her head. "Mal said she's having a fantastic time. She spends all day *reading*."

"What's wrong with that?" Mary Anne asked.

"If I couldn't get up and run outside, I'd go out of my mind," Kristy said.

Kristy, if you hadn't guessed, is very take-charge. Which is a polite way of saying she's bossy. And loud.

15

I mean those things in the nicest way. Really. I love Kristy. She is so smart and has the most amazing ideas. Amazing Idea Number One: the Baby-sitters Club. Yes, she invented us. It happened one day in seventh grade when her mom was frantically trying to line up a sitter for Kristy's little brother. Kristy wanted to help her. She realized the answer to her mom's problem — a *group* of reliable baby-sitters, like an agency, with one phone number, so parents could reach several sitters at once.

Voilà. The Baby-sitters Club was born. It started with four members and grew to seven. (Nine if you include our associate members, Logan Bruno and Shannon Kilbourne, who fill in during emergencies.) At the beginning, we did some heavy advertising, with fliers and posters in public places. Now most of the Stoneybrook parents know about us and we have lots of regular clients.

We meet on Mondays, Wednesdays, and Fridays from five-thirty to six in Claudia Kishi's bedroom. (She's the only one of us who has her own phone line, separate from the rest of her family.) It's fun, because we're close friends, but we also take sitting very seriously. For one thing, we are *always* busy with jobs. Plus we organize events for our charges, we pay dues to help cover club expenses, and we each have a title and duties.

Kristy is president. She was *born* to be a president. Don't be surprised if you see her name in a voting booth someday. She runs our meetings, she solves problems, and she thinks up most of the club events. Honestly, I don't know where she stores all her ideas. When she heard some kids complaining they were too young (or too clumsy) for T-Ball, she organized them into a softball team of her own. When she realized some of our charges had trouble adjusting to new sitters, she invented "Kid-Kits" for us to take on jobs. Kid-Kits are boxes full of our old toys, games, books, and assorted other things we scrounge up. Who would have expected kids to go crazy over them?

Kristy would.

It's easy to recognize Kristy. She's the shortest BSC member, and she's always dressed super casually. Jeans, a T-shirt or turtleneck, and sneakers — "neat and simple" is her motto. The funny thing is, her stepdad's extremely rich so she *could* buy the most expensive clothes around.

Kristy wasn't always rich. Until she was about seven, she lived across the street from Claudia with her parents and two older brothers (Charlie is now seventeen and Sam — yes, my old boyfriend — is fifteen). But her dad deserted them not long after her younger brother, David Michael, was born. (Kristy *hates* talking about her real dad.) So Mrs. Thomas raised four kids by herself *and* held down a full-time job.

Then came Watson. Watson Brewer the millionaire, that is. He fell in love with Kristy's mom and married her. Life suddenly became easier — in a way. On one hand, the Thomases moved into a mansion. On the other hand, Kristy's family doubled in size. Watson already had two kids from a previous marriage (Karen and Andrew), who live with him on alternate weekends. Then Watson and Mrs. Thomas adopted a little Vietnamese girl (Emily Michelle), and Kristy's grandmother moved in to help take care of the house and kids. Add a zoofull of pets, and you have a busy household.

"This meeting will come to order!" Kristy bellowed at the stroke of five-thirty (actually, it's more like the *click* of five-thirty on Claudia's alarm clock).

Jessi had already hung up the phone. She took her usual position on the floor. Shannon Kilbourne sat next to her. I was cross-legged on the bed, between Claudia and Mary Anne. Kristy sat forward in her director's chair. "All present and accounted for?" she asked.

"Puh-*leeze*," Claudia said with a giggle. "This isn't the army."

Kristy shrugged. "I just like the way that sounds. Any new business?"

The room fell silent for a moment. Jessi stretched out her long legs on the carpet. (She's a fabulous ballerina, so she's *always* stretching.) Her right foot disappeared under the bed, and . . . *crrrunch!*

"Oops," she said.

"The blue corn chips!" Claudia cried out. "I almost forgot about them."

Jessi pulled back her leg, and Claudia leaned down to pull a huge bag from under the bed.

"*Blue* chips?" Kristy did not look impressed. "Are they moldy?"

"No, they're made from blue corn," Claudia answered, ripping open the bag. "Try some." She gave a chip to Kristy, who held it as if it were a dead mouse.

Mary Anne reached in for some. "Dawn loved blue chips," she said with a sigh.

Dawn, by the way, is Dawn Schafer, one of our regular members. Right now she's in California, staying with her dad. She's originally from California, but when her parents divorced, Mrs. Schafer moved to Connecticut with Dawn and Dawn's brother, Jeff. Jeff never adjusted to the change and ended up moving back with his dad. Dawn stayed in Stoneybrook, but she grew incredibly homesick for "her California family," so she moved back to be with her dad and Jeff for awhile.

Dawn is also Mary Anne's stepsister and best friend. Mary Anne's been feeling pretty down since she left. (So have I. Dawn is fun to be with — plus she's the only other BSCer who doesn't eat sweets. She's a health-food freak.)

"Have you talked to her lately?" Jessi asked.

Mary Anne shook her head sadly. "Not since two nights ago."

"We could call her now if you want," Claudia offered.

Kristy looked at the clock. "Nope. It's two-thirty-four in California. She's not back from school yet." She took a fistful of chips out of the bag. "These aren't bad."

"Kristy, don't hog them," I said.

"Don't worry," Claudia assured me. "There's another bag behind my hats."

Translation: It was on the top shelf of her closet, where she keeps her huge hat collection. (Probably next to a few Milky Ways and a box of Oreos.)

Claudia is the BSC vice-president. She also happens to be my best friend in the world. I love her so much. We have a lot in common, but I will never understand her eating habits.

She loves candy, pretzels, and ice cream. Sometimes I think she's the opposite of a diabetic — her body must *need* sugar and junk. Her parents don't permit much junk food in the house, so Claudia hides candy, cookies, and chips all over her room. (Mr. and Mrs. Kishi also permit only Great Literature, so Claudia has to hide her Nancy Drew mysteries.) And here's the weirdest thing. Despite her eating habits, Claudia looks like a model and has perfect skin. She has long, jet-black hair and dark almond-shaped eyes (she's Japanese-American).

It's easy for Claud to hide stuff, because her room is a mess. Not that she's a slob. It's just that every corner is taken up by art supplies. You see, Claudia is an artist. Talk about *talent*. There's nothing she can't do well — drawing, sculpture, painting, jewelry-making. Unfortunately, art has never been very important to the Kishi family. Grades and schoolwork are, and Claudia's *not* a good student. For most of her life she felt inferior to her sister, Janine the Genius, who has enough IQ points for two people. But now even the Kishis realize Claudia's got talent.

One thing Claud and I do have in common is a passion for fashion. But our styles are different. I like sophisticated, chic clothes, and I'm great at spotting the perfect outfit in a catalog or shop window. Claudia's more *artistic*. She dresses hip and funky (hiply and funkily?), and she puts together her own outfits. For instance, at the BSC meeting she was wearing baggy wool men's pants, gathered at the waist by a black leather band; a white tuxedo shirt with rolled-up sleeves; Capezio-type flats with mismatched white and black socks; and a glittery bow-tie barrette in her hair. On someone else, the Look might be too formal, or just plain weird. On Claudia, it was fabulous.

As we sat there, passing around the second bag of chips, Shannon blurted out, "Oh! Guess what. My parents need a sitter for Tiffany and Maria on Tuesday afternoon. I have to go to this honor society meeting."

"Let's see . . ." Mary Anne looked in the club record book. "I'm at the Prezziosos', Kristy's sitting for the Hobart kids, Stacey's with Charlotte, Jessi has the Newton kids, Claudia has a dentist appointment . . . uh-oh."

Kristy shook her head. "I knew this would happen with two members missing."

"Logan adores the Hobart kids," Mary Anne said. "If he doesn't have track practice he might take your place, Kristy."

She picked up the phone and tapped out his number. After a short conversation, she hung up and said, "We're in luck!"

"Good," Kristy replied. "I'll sit for the Kilbournes."

"Bring a suit of armor," Shannon remarked. "You would not believe Tiffany. She has become such a brat."

"Really?" I said. "She used to be so quiet."

Shannon nodded. "She missed the Terrible Twos. Instead she's having the Terrible Tens. Even her teachers are complaining."

Shannon and Logan, as I mentioned before, are our two associate members, and they're not required to come to meetings. Shannon has hair to die for — blonde and curly and incredibly thick. She goes to a private school called Stoneybrook Day School, and she's involved in a lot of extracurricular activities. Lately, though, she's been picking up some of the slack for Dawn and Mallory. Logan (who is cute with a capital Q) is Mary Anne Spier's boyfriend. He's on the football and track teams, and he works part-time as a busboy, so he's often unavailable to sit.

Doesn't it figure that the quietest, shyest BSC member would be the only one with a steady boyfriend? Well, I must admit Logan has good taste. Mary Anne is also about the nicest, most sensitive and caring person I've ever met. She cries at sad movies. She cries at happy movies. Logan says she cries at store openings.

She does *not* cry over the BSC record book, which is a good thing, because the book is filled to the brim with her neat, tiny handwriting. As BSC secretary, Mary Anne keeps track of our sitting jobs in that book. She writes down all our conflicts in advance — Jessi's ballet classes, Mallory's orthodontist appointments, and whatever else comes along for the rest of us. She also keeps an updated client list, including the rates they pay and the special likes and dislikes of our charges. And she never, ever makes a mistake.

I told you how sweet-toothed Claudia and diabetic me are best friends. Well, shy Mary Anne and loudmouth Kristy are best friends, too. They are *very* different. But I can think of two things they have in common. The first is looks. Mary Anne is pretty short too, and both girls have brown hair and brown eyes.

The second thing Mary Anne has in common with Kristy is an unusual family history. Mary Anne's mom died when Mary Anne was a baby. Her dad was so overwhelmed by this that he had to send Mary Anne away to her grandparents while he recovered. When he took her back, he tried hard to be a good father *and* mother. His rules were very strict. Mary Anne had to go to bed early every night. She had to wear old-fashioned little-girl clothes and keep her hair in pigtails.

Mr. Spier changed radically, though, when he met his high-school sweetheart, who just happened to have moved back to Stoneybrook after living for years in California. (Can you guess who she is? I gave you a hint earlier.)

Yup. Mrs. Schafer, Dawn's mom. She is the opposite of Mary Anne's dad. In other words, she's wild, funny, and absentminded. Mary Anne and her dad now live in what was the Schafers' house. (It's a two-hundred-year-old farmhouse with a barn and a secret passageway to Dawn's bedroom!)

Nowadays Mary Anne looks exactly her age. She's allowed to wear the clothes of her choice and experiment with her hair and makeup.

Okay, I've told you about everyone except our junior members. Mallory Pike and Jessi are both eleven years old and in sixth grade. (The rest of us are thirteen and in eighth grade.) They have weeknight curfews, so they take mainly afternoon jobs. Since Mal came down with mono, Jessi has really missed her in meetings. They're absolutely best friends. Both of them love to read, especially horse books. Both are the oldest among their siblings, and both are convinced their parents treat them like babies.

Those are the similarities. The girls are also quite different. For one thing, Mal is Caucasian and Jessi's African-American. For another,

Jessi has two younger siblings and Mallory has seven (yes, *seven*). Mal's not a ballerina, like Jessi. She loves to write and illustrate, and she wants to be a children's book author someday.

Oh. I forgot one important thing. I'm the BSC treasurer, which means I have to collect dues every Monday. It's the least popular job, and I got it because I'm good in math. (By now I'm used to the groaning and complaints on dues day.) I figure out what part of Claud's phone bill should be paid by the club, how much money to pay Charlie Thomas (he drives Kristy to and from meetings), and whether or not we have enough leftover money for special treats, like a pizza party. I also try to keep a reserve in case we need to buy things for Kid-Kits.

Rinng!

"Hello, Baby-sitters Club!" Claudia said into the phone receiver. It was 5:38. Our first call of the afternoon had come in. The phone calls continued, almost nonstop, until six o'clock. We hardly had time to talk about anything — including my upcoming date.

It was just as well, I thought. The school year was still young. Who knew what could happen? No use building it up.

I had a daydream, though. I imagined a championship game in the SMS gym, standing room only. I saw Stoneybrook behind by one point and RJ scoring a basket with one second left in the game. I heard a deafening roar as RJ bounded off the court and lifted me into his arms.

I had to laugh. It was ridiculous. I didn't even know the guy.

Oh, well, a girl can dream, can't she?

CHAPTER 3

On Friday I made myself three promises.

1. I would not mention my date to anyone at school or at the BSC meeting.

2. If I were asked about it, I would change the subject quickly.

3. If and when I saw RJ, I would remain cool and calm.

How did I do? A big, fat 0 for 3.

I blabbered about how excited I was to Sheila McGregor in homeroom. When Mary Anne asked me how I was feeling, I shrieked in the hallway. Then RJ decided to sit at our table during lunch, and I could hardly put a sentence together. It didn't help that I was eating a sandwich on a poppy-seed roll, so I looked as if I had gaps between my teeth. (Kristy made sure to let me know about it — *afterward*, of course.)

By the end of school I was a wreck. I almost forgot to go to the BSC meeting. I showed up at 5:37 and guess what they were talking about?

My date. We ended up discussing the time RJ was picking me up (six-thirty), our destination (downtown), our "agenda" (a movie and then a bite to eat), and what I was going to wear (a black-and-white plaid unitard with a tankstyle top, covered with a black, over-sized cotton knit jersey).

What else did we do at the meeting? Don't ask me. My mind was in the ozone layer. I think I agreed to take a sitting job, but I'm not sure. All I know was that at six on the nose, I was out like a shot.

Because of my diabetes, I have to eat meals at regular times. Since RJ and I were going straight to the movie, that meant I needed to have dinner beforehand. I arrived home at 6:06, so I had exactly twenty-four minutes in which to eat and get ready.

I was glad I'd decided what to wear in advance. I ran straight to my room, changed, and put on a little makeup. Mom and I wolfed down some salad and leftover lasagna.

As I was drinking a glass of juice, the doorbell rang.

I coughed. Some juice had caught in my throat.

"Take it easy, sweetheart," Mom said with a smile.

"I'm — " *Cough.* "I'm — " *Cough.* "I'm all right." I swallowed and took a deep breath. "I'll get it."

Calmly I stood up from the table. Mom was giving me a very patient smile. I went to the front door and opened it — not too eager, but friendly. "Hi, RJ!" I said.

Hic.

I tried to swallow the hiccup, but I couldn't. It just snuck up my windpipe. I was horrified. I wanted to melt into the carpet.

"Can you stand on your head?" RJ asked.

"Huh?" Great. I was hiccuping like a frog, and RJ wanted to do gymnastics in the living room. "Uh, yeah, but . . ."

Hic.

"It's how you get rid of hiccups," RJ said.

"Here, drink this." Mom, the voice of reason, walked up behind me with a glass of water. I swallowed it slowly.

RJ shook his head. "Nah, standing on your head is definitely better."

I managed a smile. "It's okay. Really. They're gone."

Have you ever actually forced down a hiccup? I did. It wasn't fun. It felt as if a tiny bomb had gone off in my stomach. But I was *not* going to be talked into doing headstands on a first date in a beautiful new outfit.

Mom cheerfully waved good-bye as RJ and

I slid into the car. Mr. Blaser was driving. He was a bigger version of RJ — tall, broad-shouldered, and handsome.

How was the ride? Well, we started by talking about the cold winter weather. That was okay. But it led to a very long discussion about the right kind of antifreeze for the Blasers' car. RJ and his father both had strong opinions. Me? I understood a little bit of it, mainly words like *and*, *the*, and *bottle*. I nodded a lot.

Fortunately, we reached the theatre before the conversation became too unbearable. We went straight to the box office, bought tickets, and stood on the popcorn line.

"Hey, great, they have caramel corn!" RJ exclaimed.

"Um, I'll have regular," I said.

"Your choice. I'll get one of each. I guess you're on a *diet*, huh?" He said "diet" in a mocking tone of voice.

"Yeah, I am, sort of," I replied.

RJ smiled and rolled his eyes. "Girls." He sighed. "Diet soda, too?"

"Thanks," I said.

Okay, okay, I chickened out. I admit it. I didn't want to tell RJ about my diabetes. Some people get grossed out by the mention of it. Why spoil the date so early? I'd mention it when we got to know each other better.

The theatre was busy, and we had to maneuver our way through a crowd to get to the door.

I saw a few familiar faces. Sabrina Bouvier and her date were talking to some friends by a water fountain. Erica Blumberg, Cokie Mason, and a bunch of their friends were in line for the restroom.

You know what? They all, *all* stared at me.

You know what else? It felt wonderful. I slipped my arm into RJ's, and he gave me a huge grin.

The theater was noisy and crowded as we walked in, but in the last few rows were plenty of empty seats. "Want to sit back here?" I asked.

"It's kind of far away," RJ said. "There are seats up front."

There were — in the first two rows. "Those are too close," I replied.

"Okay, no problem."

RJ marched to the center of the theater. One row was not quite full, with two single seats separated by three couples. "Yo," RJ called out, "can you guys move over so we can sit together?"

I couldn't believe he was doing this. All six people had to get up and move, muttering and fumbling with their winter clothes. I felt awfully guilty.

We squeezed by everyone, took off our coats, and sat in our seats.

"This okay?" RJ asked.

It wasn't. The guy to my left was hogging the armrest. In front of me was a girl with major hair. She was either six feet tall or was sitting on her coat. The only place to hold my coat was in my lap, which was also the only place to hold my popcorn and drink. "It's fine," I answered.

"I hear this movie is really funny," RJ said. "Marty saw it."

"I like Todd Byron," I replied, mentioning one of the stars. "He's a great actor, even in serious movies. Did you see *My Only Girl?*"

RJ shook his head. "Uh-uh. I guess I like movies that make me laugh, you know? And they have to have a *plot*."

"I know what you mean. I like mysteries. Did you see — "

"Also action films," RJ barged on. "Car chases and stuff. I like them. I don't know why, I just do. You sure you don't want some of this?" He held out the caramel corn.

"No, thanks."

RJ shrugged, stared at the blank screen, and started munching away. I took a handful of my popcorn.

Everyone seemed to be talking but us. I hate

when I'm getting to know someone and the conversation goes nowhere. I don't know whether to feel bored or boring. "So," I said, "who are you playing tomorrow?"

Ta da. RJ came to life. Talking about basketball, he was funny and easygoing. He was explaining something called sudden-death overtime when *Mall Warriors II* began.

I hadn't seen *Mall Warriors I*, and I was a little concerned I might have missed something.

Well, I didn't need to worry. A three-year-old could have followed the plot. It was about a group of teens who booby-trap a mall to catch a pair of world-famous mall thieves.

Personally, I found it amazingly dumb. I couldn't wait for it to end. But RJ laughed a lot. This was not a good sign.

After it was finally over, RJ turned to me with a huge smile and said, "What did you think?"

Under my down coat, I was sweaty. My neck hurt from craning to see around the hair mountain in front of me. The movie hadn't made my top-ten list by a longshot. And I'd spent two hours deciding that RJ and I had nothing in common.

I had to be honest. "I didn't really like it," I said.

RJ's face was a little curious, a little concerned, and (I think) a little annoyed. "Yeah? Oh, that's too bad, Stace. You should have told me. We could have snuck out."

"It's okay, RJ. I mean, I still had fun — " Okay, I was stretching it.

"Hey, I'm starving. Let's get something to eat," RJ suggested, his face suddenly brightening. "How about Pizza Express?"

I have about three or four favorite places to eat in Stoneybrook. Pizza Express is not one of them. (It's *okay*. It's just not my fav.) But I was dying to get out of that theater. "Sure," I said.

In the lobby, RJ called his dad to let him know where we were going. I stretched my legs and let myself air out.

Sabrina saw me again and waved. She had that envious look in her eyes. Somehow, it didn't affect me the way it had earlier. I was busy evaluating my date. I gave it a 3 on a scale of 1 (worst) to 10 (best). RJ was okay in some ways, but I had a feeling we weren't made for each other.

I felt depressed as we walked out of the theater. I guess I had built the date up too much in advance.

Well, guess who was in Pizza Express that night? The Group. Just about the entire cheerleading squad and the basketball team, taking up four tables and having a great time.

"Hey, Blasemeister!" Marty Bukowski called out to RJ.

"The Bukeman!" RJ returned.

RJ took my arm and we walked to Marty's table. Everyone turned to us and said hi. I have never seen so many toothpaste-ad smiles in my life. Sheila was pulling over a couple of chairs from a nearby empty table.

Boy, was my mood changing. A few days earlier, none of these kids would have given me a second look. Now they were moving aside to let me sit down.

RJ did a few high-fives and low-fives, then introduced me all around. No one seemed to care how loud we were, not even the owner of Pizza Express. In fact, as we sat down he personally came over to take our orders.

"So," Sheila whispered, "did you have a good time?"

I glanced at RJ, who was deep in conversation with another player across the table, Robert Brewster. In a low voice, I said, "Yeah, except the movie was kind of dumb."

"Sometimes that's better," she said with a giggle.

I knew what she was implying. She figured RJ and I had spent the whole time kissing.

I didn't know how to answer her. Would I sound dorky if I said nothing had happened?

Maybe I was *supposed* to have been kissing RJ. Maybe he brought me to a bad movie on purpose, so our attention wouldn't be distracted from each other.

But he hadn't even *tried* to kiss me. I wondered why. Was I that boring? Did he find that awful movie more interesting than I was? Should I have made the first move?

Easy, Stacey, I told myself. This is not a big deal.

"I didn't like that movie either," announced Corinne Baker, who was sitting next to Robert across the table. "Sequels are never as good as originals."

"Never," I agreed.

"Also the acting seemed, like, amateurish," Corinne continued.

"Exactly," I said.

Sheila shrugged. "I didn't notice. I was too busy watching Todd Byron — or else I had my eyes closed."

She giggled, and Marty gave her ribs a nudge.

"Shei*la*," Corinne scolded. "You don't have to embarrass Stacey!"

"I'm not embarrassed," I replied.

"Corinne, I'm sure she's kissed guys before," Sheila said. "Right, Stacey?"

"Sure," I answered. (Yes, it's true.)

Corinne seemed surprised. "Oh. It's just that — well, I didn't think the girls in your . . . you know, *crowd* — "

"What do you mean?" I asked.

"You *know*," Corinne went on. "Those girls you hang with. The baby-sitters. Some of them are so young."

I realized she'd seen me with Jessi and Mallory in school. "Well, a couple of them are, but most of us are eighth-graders."

"Uh-huh." Corinne didn't sound impressed.

"Don't be such a snot, Corinne," Sheila snapped. "I mean, we all go through that stage. You did, too."

That stage? Was I going through a stage? Was baby-sitting something you grew out of? I never thought of it that way. Older girls baby-sat.

Before I could say anything, the pizza arrived. "Help yourself, guys," RJ offered to the others. "We can always order another."

RJ, Marty, Robert, and I all reached for slices. My piece and Robert's were stuck together. As we pulled them apart, the cheese made a gooey bridge.

"Oops!" Robert laughed as he pulled the cheese apart.

Whoa.

Cute Alert. Four alarms.

I hadn't taken a close look at his face before. He had dark brown hair that fell over his forehead, dimples, and a smile that should have had a DANGER sign on it.

I smiled and looked away. I didn't want Corinne to think I was after Robert. She was sitting next to him, so I figured they were together.

Well, Robert's eyes stayed on mine much longer than mine did on his. (Hmmmm . . .)

"Uh-oh, look who's coming," Marty murmured.

Jason Fox, who's in my math class, was walking toward us with two friends. "Hey, guys, good luck with the game tomorrow night."

"Thanks, buddy," RJ said.

Jason nodded and raised his fist in the air. "We're number one! Yeah!"

As he left the restaurant, Sheila burst into giggles. "What a dork."

"Hey," RJ said, "leave him alone. He comes to all the games."

Margie Greene leaned over from the next table. "Yeah, and stares at all of us. He doesn't care about *basketball*."

"Are you going to be there, Stace?" Corinne asked.

"I wouldn't miss it!" I said. "The whole — all my friends will be there." I had almost said *the whole Baby-sitters Club*, but decided against it.

"We'll be doing some new cheers," Sheila explained. "Tell us if you like them."

"Okay."

"Carbo-loading, eh, guys?" boomed the voice of Mr. Blake, an SMS teacher.

"Yo, Mr. Blake!" Marty stood and gave him a high-five.

"I guess I found the place where the stars eat, huh?" Mr. Blake remarked.

We laughed. All of us "stars."

My rating for the night was rising. So what if the date hadn't been perfect?

It felt good to be in the limelight.

CHAPTER 4

"*A tisket! A tasket!*
Put it in the basket!
Who's the best? SMS!
Yeeeaaaa, team!"

I'd never been so excited about a sports event. Just hearing the cheerleaders practice made my heart flutter.

It was Saturday night, about fifteen minutes before the game. Mary Anne, Logan, Jessi, Kristy, and I had just walked into the gym. We were going to watch the game, then us girls were going to have a sleepover at Kristy's.

My friends were calm and happy. Me? I was a wreck.

Maybe it was because I actually *knew* everyone on the basketball court now. I was feeling nervous for them.

Sheila was perfecting her split. Darcy was figuring out moves with Penny Weller. RJ and Malik were shooting balls a zillion feet away from the basket — and getting them in. Robert was dribbling another ball while Marty tried to bat it away. (What an expression — *dribbling*. You expect to see a trail of saliva. Why don't they just say "bouncing"?)

The gym was starting to fill up. Logan found seats for us near midcourt. I tried to catch Sheila's eye, but she'd started talking to Marty. The two of them looked soooo in love.

I pictured myself in her place. Imagine some big hunkified guy singling me out like that, in front of hundreds of people.

Sigh.

My eyes moved right to Robert. I don't know why.

"Chips? Malted milk balls?" Leave it to Claudia. She was already offering us junk food. Her shoulder bag was crammed with it.

"Thanks," I said, taking a bag of pretzels.

Corinne looked our way, just as I was stuffing my face. I waved and she gave me a smile.

I could see her eyes move from Jessi to Claudia to Kristy to Mary Anne, then quickly look away. Suddenly I didn't want those pretzels anymore.

I wondered what Corinne was thinking. What would *I* have thought if I were Corinne? Claud was rummaging around for snacks, wearing an outfit that suddenly seemed a little weird (a sequined vest over a man's white shirt and bell-bottomed spandex pants). Kristy was gesturing around the court with a potato-chip bag as she lectured Mary Anne about the rules of basketball. Mary Anne looked pale and washed-out (and bored) in the bright lights. And Jessi — well, Jessi was acting like an eleven-year-old.

"This is so cool," she squealed. "I hope it goes into overtime so I can stay up *really* late."

Now, there's nothing wrong with saying something like that. I'd have felt the same way at that age.

But somehow it bothered me — just the way our pigging out did, and Claudia's outfit, and Kristy's lecturing.

I shrugged it off. After all, your friends are your friends. Why should I be ashamed of them? That would be true snobbishness, and I was *not* going to behave that way!

Before long the players left the court. The cheerleaders sat on a bench, and the gym quieted down. Then a voice over the loudspeaker boomed out: *"Welcome to Stoneybrook Middle School, ladies and gentlemen! Tonight the SMS Chargers will play the Sheridan Wildcats!"*

Well, I thought I would lose my hearing. The gym exploded with cheers.

It turned out to be the first explosion of many. What an exciting game! Sheridan was a good team, better than we'd expected.

Whenever they were ahead of SMS, I felt my stomach knot up. Then the cheerleaders would go wild. The rest of us would join in their cheers, at the top of our lungs. Even Mary Anne was screaming.

By halftime I was hoarse. My shin ached, too. I had banged it during a huge group hug with my friends, when RJ got a basket right at the buzzer.

The second half? Oh my lord, talk about *tense*. Neither team could keep the lead. Sheridan pulled ahead, then Stoneybrook. My fingernails were ragged. My stomach was a mess. I thought Kristy was going to have a heart attack. Mary Anne almost cried a couple of times.

I was having "deep identification." That's what my English teacher would have called it. She's always asking if we *identify* with any characters in the books we're reading. I feel so frustrated when I don't. Well, during this game I was identifying like crazy. When Marty fell and hurt his ankle, I grimaced. When Robert made a basket from far away, I felt ecstatic. And the cheerleaders? I think I'd memorized every move. I could swear my legs hurt from *their* splits.

Toward the end of the game, the players began losing their tempers. RJ collided with a

Sheridan player and started a fight. Robert had to pull RJ away and calm him down. The SMS coach, Mr. Halvorsen, got into a shouting match with the referee. With three seconds to go, the game was tied.

What happened next? A Sheridan player threw the ball, Wayne McConville grabbed it and passed it to Malik. Malik threw it and . . . SWISH!

"Game is over! Stoneybrook is the winner by ONE POINT!" Whoever was on the loudspeaker was practically shrieking.

You would have thought it was the end of the championships. The stands emptied. We poured out onto the court. It was pandemonium. Absolute, total, utter chaos. Even teachers and parents were hugging each other and screaming. I could see Mr. Blake clapping Malik on the back. RJ and Robert had lifted Wayne McConville onto their shoulders. Marty ran to Sheila and swept her off her feet (literally). The rest of the cheerleaders had given up doing organized cheers. They were just jumping up and down, flinging their pom-poms around. Jason Fox was performing a little victory dance under the basket.

I ran up to Darcy, who was the nearest cheerleader. "Congratulations!" I called out.

She didn't hear me over the noise.

That was when Robert passed by. He and Wayne were talking and laughing. "Robert!" I yelled.

"Oh, hi!" (Wow, was that smile a killer.) "Good game, huh?"

"You were great!" I replied.

"Thanks."

I did it. I hugged him. I didn't plan it, it just happened. It didn't *mean* anything, really. Everybody was hugging. Besides, he was so sweaty it was kind of gross.

But only kind of.

As he disappeared into the crowd, I looked around for Corinne. She was nowhere to be seen. Whew.

I tried to elbow my way closer to the cheerleaders, but it was hopeless. An enormous crowd had formed around them and the players.

I hung out on the edge of the throng, babbling away with anyone I knew. After awhile, people began to leave. I found myself inching closer to Robert, who was now wiping his face with a towel and talking to the coach.

Phweeeeeet!

A piercing whistle rang out from the stands. The noise level dropped. Faces turned toward the sound.

It was Kristy, standing about halfway up the bleachers, looking directly at me. "Stacey, are you coming to the sleepover or not?" she yelled. "Charlie's outside with the van!"

Gulp.

I could hear snickering. Someone said, "A sleepover? Oh, goody!" in a childish voice.

I was cringing. I was melting.

Thank you, Kristy Thomas.

But what could I do? I *did* want to go to the sleepover. I nodded nonchalantly to Kristy and began heading for the door.

On my way out, I did not dare look in the direction of the cheerleaders. Or Robert.

I brooded all the way to Kristy's. But I got over it. Especially when I saw Watson in the kitchen wearing a tall chef's hat and a spotless apron. He was carrying a rolling pin in one hand, a kitchen knife in the other, and a huge grin was on his face.

On the table was the hugest spread of food you ever saw — sliced cold cuts, loaves of bread, veggies and dip, and fresh fruit.

Our mouths dropped open. We were *ravenous*. It took all I could do to keep from . . . well, dribbling.

"That's beautiful!" Claudia exclaimed.

"*You* made this?" Kristy looked absolutely shocked.

Watson raised an eyebrow. "Hey, it was a tough job, but somebody had to do it."

Kristy's mother breezed in. "Hey, kids, how was the — " She took a look at Watson, then us, and burst into laughter.

"What's so funny?" Kristy asked. "Look at all the work Watson did — "

"Yeah," Mrs. Brewer said between giggles. "He really strained his fingers calling the deli on the phone and placing the order!"

Watson grinned and shrugged.

"Ooooh . . ." With a sly smile, Kristy picked up a strawberry and reared back as if to throw it.

"Okay!" Watson cried. "I'm out of here!"

We were cracking up. I always thought Watson was bland and serious, but I guess everyone has a goofy side.

Anyway, we dug in to the platter. The food was delicious (and nothing was sugary — thank you, Watson). We gabbed a mile a minute about the game. We laughed, we gossiped, we made a total mess.

It turned out to be one of our best sleepovers ever. And I realized something. I had some of the best friends ever.

CHAPTER 5

Sheila was standing outside homeroom on Monday morning. So were Darcy and Penny. They were looking at me with humongous smiles, as if they'd been waiting for me.

Darcy and Penny were not in my homeroom. I had no idea what they were doing there.

As I walked closer, they turned to each other and giggled.

Uh-oh.

They were going to torment me. That's what this was all about. They were going to laugh about the sleepover. I almost ran off.

But no. I held my chin high. If they were going to act that way, I'd just march right past them into the room.

"Stacey, you are going to *die*!" Sheila exclaimed.

Huh?

I stood there, staring. I must have looked

like a department-store mannequin.

They started giggling again. Sheila whispered to Darcy, "You tell her."

"Why do I have to?" Darcy replied.

"She's *your* friend, Sheila," Penny said.

"You guys are such bàbies!" Sheila exhaled with frustration. "Okay. Come here, Stacey. I don't want the whole world to know."

I walked over to them. They looked as if they were ready to burst with excitement.

"Robert likes you," Sheila said.

My brain did not handle the sentence. It was as if Sheila had said, "Your hair is blue," or "Yesterday is tomorrow," or "Life is a cheeseburger." No logic, no sense.

"What?" was my response.

Giggles again.

"He noticed you on Friday night," Darcy said. "At the Pizza Express."

"Remember, when your slices stuck together?" Sheila added.

"Love at first bite!" Penny covered her mouth and laughed at her own joke.

"Well — but — how — " My brain was now rediscovering the English language, but slowly. "What about Corinne?" I finally asked.

"What about her?" Penny asked.

"Robert is interested in her, isn't he?"

The girls exchanged a knowing glance. "*Cor-*

inne is the only one who thinks Robert is interested in her," Darcy replied.

Robert? Interested in me? Oh, please. He didn't know me. I wasn't one of The Group.

"His dad gave a bunch of us a ride home that night," Sheila said. "I was the last person he dropped off, so Robert and I had a few minutes in the car together. We were talking about the game, and then he said to me, and I quote, 'You seem to know Stacey pretty well. Is she going steady with RJ?' Just like that, out of the clear blue sky." Sheila paused for effect. I caught my breath. "Now, I didn't know the answer for sure. But I remembered you said you didn't like the movie. And I got the feeling you guys didn't . . . you know . . . kiss or anything. And you and RJ weren't exactly *acting* like lovebirds. So I decided to tell him you weren't. Was that okay?"

"I wasn't what?" I asked.

"Going steady with RJ!" Sheila answered with exasperation. "You're not, are you?"

"No!" I answered too loudly. I could feel myself blushing. "I mean, you were right to say that."

"Lucky," Penny said. "Robert is a real nine-one-one."

I looked at her blankly. "A nine-one-one?"

"You've never heard that expression?" She

shook her head in disbelief. "It's like calling nine-one-one because you're about to die from excitement? You know?"

"Right," I said. (I guessed that was a "Group" expression.)

"Well, I don't blame him," Sheila remarked. "He has good taste."

"Oh, groan," Darcy said. Then she looked at me and added quickly, "Really, he's also the nicest guy, Stacey. Sometimes the good-looking ones are jerks, but Robert's different."

"Anyway, I said he should call you," Sheila added. "And he said he would. So be prepared."

Boy, was I smiling. "You guys, I don't know what to say. Thanks for telling me."

"That's what friends are for," Sheila replied with a warm smile.

Darcy looked at her watch. "Oops, almost time for our practice," she said to Penny. Both girls laughed. I didn't get the joke.

"Sheila," Penny said, "did you tell Stacey about . . . you know what?"

I laughed. "Another secret?"

"Well, not exactly a *secret*," Penny replied. "It's just that one of the cheerleaders is moving. We're going to hold tryouts to replace her, but we haven't set a date. We figured we'd let you know early, in case you want to start working out."

"If you're interested," Darcy added.

"Me?" I squeaked.

"Why not?" Sheila asked.

"Well, I don't know."

"You're definitely pretty enough to be on the squad," Darcy went on. "You just have to know how to do the usual stuff — splits, jumps, cartwheels — plus be able to pick up a combination."

"Splits?" I said. Just thinking about them hurt. And what did she mean, I was *pretty* enough to be on the squad?

"Splits aren't as hard as you think," Darcy said. "Besides, you have plenty of time to practice."

Riinnnnggg!

"Uh-oh! See you!" Penny cried.

She and Darcy raced away. Sheila practically had to pull me into homeroom.

It was a good thing she did, too. Otherwise I might have stood in the hall for hours.

I was in a daze. *Me*, Stacey McGill, a cheerleader? How weird. How . . . fabulous!

Here's why it was weird: I'd never seen real live cheerleaders before I came to Stoneybrook. My school in New York City didn't have them. Cheerleading was frowned on. Girls preferred having their own teams to cheering for the boys.

That always made sense to me. It still does.

Besides, pleated skirts, pom-poms, and white bucks are not exactly my style.

But let's face facts. What's cool in one place is not necessarily cool in another. And being a cheerleader in Stoneybrook was definitely cool. Just being friends with the cheerleaders made me feel good.

And if I became a cheerleader — just *if* — I could be closer to Robert.

I spent the rest of the morning on a cloud. I wondered how hard those cheerleading moves were. In gym class, before we started exercises, I quietly went into a corner and tried to do a split.

There's a good reason they call it a split. Wow, did it hurt. If I was going to try out, I would need to work *hard*.

I decided to keep quiet about tryouts. I would practice a little, maybe ask someone to help me. If I turned out to be too much of a klutz, I would just skip tryouts, no harm done.

I did not mention anything to the other members of the BSC at lunch. I wanted to tell them about Robert, but what if he never called me? *That* would be awkward.

So I was Silent Stacey for the rest of the day, even though my heart was pounding.

When I got home, I could barely concentrate

on my homework. I was in the middle of a math problem when the phone rang.

My hand tightened. I broke the point on my pencil. My chair almost fell over as I ran to the phone.

"Hello!" I cried, feeling like a balloon ready to burst.

"Good afternoon, this is the Cine-Home Pay Cable Network," said a voice. "This month we're offering a free hook-up to new subscribers. . . ."

Fffffffff. I could feel my air slowly leaking out. I called my mom at work, and asked her to take care of the call.

A few minutes later the phone rang again. This time it was Claudia, asking if she could borrow a barrette.

Call Number Three was from one of Mom's friends.

Calls Number Four and Five were for Rupert Peebles. We get his calls from time to time. Mom figured out that he must have been the person who had our phone number before we did.

I started my math homework at 4:30. Now, math is my very favorite subject, but by 5:24, I was still staring at the third problem (of twenty). It was the absolute latest I could remain in the house and still reach the BSC meeting in time.

I ran downstairs, found my coat, and raced out the door.

I was halfway to the sidewalk when I heard . . . *rinnnnnng.*

It was 5:26. Kristy was going to kill me if I was late for the meeting. Nevertheless, you know in those Road Runner cartoons, when you hear a *pshoooo* sound and the Road Runner disappears in a cloud of dust? Well, that was me. I was in the house instantly.

I ran to the kitchen. I stopped by the phone and collected myself. Then I calmly picked up the receiver and dropped it.

Clunk!

I scooped it off the floor. "Hello?" I said. "Sorry!"

I heard the most wonderful laugh on the other end of the phone. "That's okay, I have another ear."

It was Robert! I didn't know whether to laugh or cry. "Hi, Robert," was the only brilliant reply I could think of.

"Hi. What a game Saturday, huh?"

"It was *great*! Especially that . . . that jump shot you made near the end! You're very good."

Robert laughed again. "Well, not as good as Malik or Wayne. Those guys are naturals. I have to work hard to do half what they do."

Cute *and* modest. What a rare combination

in a boy. "Well, you looked pretty good to me," I said.

"Thanks. So did you — I mean, you know, it was great to see you."

"Uh-huh. Me, too. It was great to see you." This conversation was painful. I sounded like a parrot.

"So, um, I guess you'll come to the next game, too?"

"Sure," I replied.

"Hey, great. I'll see you there."

That was *it*? He called to see if I was coming to the game? I tried not to sound disappointed. "Okay. Well, see you."

"Um, wait. I was just thinking. I'm not really doing anything Friday night. I mean, I know you probably are, but — "

"No, I'm not," I shot back.

"No? Well, maybe we could, like, get together or something. You know, see a movie."

"Not *Mall Warriors II*," I said.

Robert laughed again. "That's the last movie I'd see!"

"Oh, good!" I was so grateful. We had something in common already. I could tell we were going to get along.

"So, is six-thirty okay? I'll ask one of my parents to drive."

"Great," I said.

"Okay, well, 'bye."

" 'Bye."

The moment I hung up, I screamed. Then I called Mom at work again. I told her what had happened. She seemed delighted.

Delighted was too tame a word for how I felt. I glided out of the house. I knew that five-thirty was in the distant past. I knew Kristy was probably fuming.

But at that moment, I couldn't have cared less. As I headed for Claudia's, my feet barely touched the ground.

CHAPTER 6

Tuesday

Your little sister has really changed, Shannon. No offense, but I thought Maria was going to turn out to be a bookworm. All of a sudden she's outgoing and athletic.

Tiffany's a good kid, too. But put the two of them together — whoa. I felt like a referee, not a baby-sitter....

It was the day after Robert had asked me out. I had told everyone in the BSC what had happened, and they were thrilled. Unfortunately, it was also the day Kristy had her first sitting job with Tiffany and Maria Kilbourne.

Kristy is a great sitter. Fun-loving but firm. Kids like her and she can match their incredible energy. But even Kristy had trouble with Tiffany and Maria.

Although Shannon is a BSC member, none of us knows the Kilbourne family very well. They live in Kristy's neighborhood, and the girls go to a private school. So their circle of friends is different.

I've already told you a little about Shannon. She is a real Achiever. She's in the honor society, she acts and sings in plays, and she's practically fluent in Spanish and French.

Tiffany is a ten-year-old version of Shannon — physically, at least. She has the same curly blonde hair, blue eyes, and high cheekbones. Maria has dark, reddish-brown hair and hazel eyes. To tell you the truth, they almost don't look like sisters.

Kristy had met Maria many times before. (Occasionally Maria comes to the Brewer house to play with Karen.)

As for Tiffany? Well, Kristy figured she'd be like Maria — shy, studious, and polite. Or like

Shannon — bright, fun, and thoughtful. Either way, she expected Tiffany and Maria to be two nice, easy kids. Sitting for them would be a dream job.

That image lasted until Kristy rang the front doorbell.

"I'll get it!" a voice shouted from behind the closed door. *Thump-thump-thump-thump* came the sound of footsteps down stairs.

"Get out of my way!" Another voice.

"Hey, stop!" The first voice.

"You're so slow!"

"Mo-om!"

"Baby!"

"Don't call me that!"

"What?"

"Baby!"

"Okay, *baby!*"

"Girls, will you please stop!" Whew. A grown-up voice. Finally.

"She started it!"

"She pushed me!"

"She was being slow!"

"She called me baby!"

Uh-oh.

Suddenly Kristy wished she hadn't volunteered for this job. She could tell it was going to be a long, long day.

The door lurched open. Mrs. Kilbourne gave Kristy a wide, beaming smile. (Of course. *She* was the one who was leaving.) "Well, hello, Kristy! Come on in."

Clutching her Kid-Kit, Kristy walked inside. She saw the two girls at the foot of the living room stairs. They stood there like statues, the goddesses of Gloom and Doom.

Kristy said hi.

Gloom and Doom grunted.

Mrs. Kilbourne led Kristy into the kitchen and gave her instructions. The last thing she said was, "Make sure Tiffany starts her homework before dinner." Then she got her coat, kissed her daughters, and breezed out the doorway.

Kristy could have sworn she heard a sigh of relief.

"So," Kristy said. "Want to go outside before you start your homework? There's plenty of snow for a snowperson."

No reply.

"No, huh? Well, that's okay." Kristy set down her Kid-Kit and began to open it. "Maybe we can find something in here."

The girls leaned forward to look. Kristy pulled out an old rag doll, some dinosaur figurines, and a few small puzzle books.

"Ooh, word searches!" Maria cried out. "I *love* those." She reached for one of the books and a pencil.

Tiffany crinkled her nose. "That's baby stuff." She rummaged around and pulled out an old yo-yo.

Maria sat on the floor next to the coffee table. As she opened the book and began working on a puzzle, Tiffany experimented with the yo-yo.

Kristy was proud of herself. She settled onto the couch.

"Sub . . . ma . . . rine," Maria muttered, circling a diagonal word in a puzzle.

Tiffany was swinging the yo-yo in an arc now. She was also moving closer to her sister.

"Ooh! Tug . . . boat!" Maria said. "Look! I got them all!"

Whack. The yo-yo smacked Maria on her elbow. *"Owww!"* She whirled around. "You did that on purpose!"

Tiffany rolled her eyes. "Yeah, right."

"Uh, Tiffany," Kristy said. "That's a little close. Maybe you could do that in another room?"

"Let's go to the TV room," Tiffany replied. "Can you teach me some tricks?"

"Sure." Kristy looked over at Maria. "You okay in here by yourself?"

"Kan . . . ga . . . roo," Maria mumbled.

Tiffany led Kristy into a large, wood-paneled room just past the kitchen. A long Haitiancotton couch faced a huge TV set. Next to the TV was a cabinet with glass shelves above and drawers below.

Kristy noticed a few trophies and awards on the shelves, so she stepped closer to look. The top two shelves were obviously Shannon's — a drama plaque, a framed honor society certificate, and an archery trophy from summer camp, among others. The third shelf held a few swimming trophies. " 'League of Independent Schools Athletics, Swimming, Elementary Division, First-Place Butterfly,' " Kristy read. "Is this yours?"

Tiffany exhaled impatiently. "Read the *name!*"

"Oh." Sure enough, *Maria Kilbourne* was engraved at the bottom of the plaque. "Wow. I didn't know she was a swimmer," said Kristy.

"Can you teach me the yo-yo stuff now?" Tiffany asked impatiently.

"Oh! Sorry." Kristy reached for the yo-yo. "Do you know 'Walking the Dog'?"

Maria's voice responded with, "Did you see the one for school record in the breaststroke?"

Kristy turned to see Maria peeking in the room. Beaming, she ran to the case.

Tiffany slumped onto the couch. "Bo-ring!"

"Jealous." Maria stuck out her tongue. She opened the case and took out a gaudy plastic trophy.

"Maria, I am impressed!" Kristy said. "I remember you used to *hate* athletic things."

Maria beamed. "I did! But now I love swimming. My coach says I'm a natural. I even got a write-up in the Stoneybrook Day School newspaper!" She reached into the top drawer and pulled out the article.

"You are so conceited!" Tiffany snapped. She leaped up and grabbed the article. "Kristy was teaching me something."

Maria held tight to her end of the paper. "Give me that!"

Rrrrrrip!

Each sister now held half an article. "Look what you did!" Maria cried.

"What's the difference, *baby*? You have a hundred and three copies of it!"

"Don't call me that!"

"Whoa! Truce!" Kristy called out. She had reached the end of her patience. "Okay, look. Maybe you two need to get out of each other's hair. Why don't you go upstairs and start your homework — peacefully, in your own rooms. Uh, do you have separate rooms?"

"Yeah," Maria replied. "Want to see?"

"Sure." Anything to get them upstairs, Kristy thought.

She followed Maria up the steps. Halfway there, she turned around. "Tiffany? Are you coming?"

"I don't want to do my homework! You didn't teach me those yo-yo tricks, like you said you would."

"Okay, okay. If I come down and teach you, *then* will you do your homework?"

Tiffany said something under her breath. It didn't sound like yes.

At the top of the stairway, Maria led Kristy down a hallway, then proudly showed off her room. It had pink wallpaper with a heart pattern, and stuffed animals were propped up all over the place. Framed swim team photos hung over her desk. Another swimming trophy sat on her dresser. "That's for the side stroke. I just got it yesterday."

As Maria sat down at her desk, Kristy said, "Let me know if you need anything. I'll get your sister."

"She won't come," Maria replied. "She never does her homework. She is so bad in school."

"Come on, that's not nice."

"It's true. The teacher sends her home with notes sometimes. Mom and Dad get really mad. Last time they took away her allowance. So that's why she's not — "

Maria's eyes widened and she cut herself off.

"Not what?" Kristy asked.

"Nothing."

66

Kristy raised her presidential eyebrow. "Mariaaaaa."

Maria looked at the floor. "Tiffany got another note today. She told me. But she's not going to give it to Mom and Dad."

"Maria!" Tiffany's voice boomed from downstairs. "I'm going to kill you! I told you not to tell — "

"She made me!" Maria gave Kristy an angry and frightened look. "See what you did!"

WHACK! The TV room door slammed shut.

Kristy took a deep breath. "Sorry, Maria," she said. "I'll go talk to her. It'll be all right."

She left Maria's room and walked through the hallway. She caught a glimpse of Shannon's room — a Stoneybrook Day pennant on the wall, neat stacks of books on the desk, and a poster from a summer camp production of *Oklahoma!*

Just opposite it was another room. Kristy couldn't help stopping when she saw what was inside.

It was a pigsty. Papers, books, pillows, and plastic wrappers covered the floor. The bed was unmade, and the desk was buried under notebooks, paperbacks, CDs, cassettes, you name it.

No wonder Tiffany doesn't want to do her homework, Kristy thought. She needs a snowplow just to get to her desk.

And every time she *does* go upstairs, she has to deal with an older sister who's Ms. Star Student and a younger sister who has suddenly become a Future Olympian. Being a normal kid in a family like that couldn't be easy.

With a sigh, Kristy went downstairs. She wasn't angry at Tiffany now.

Slowly she pushed open the TV room door. Tiffany was flumped on the couch, arms folded, in her own storm cloud.

"I didn't forget about 'Walking the Dog,' you know," said Kristy.

"Go away." Tiffany shifted so her back was toward Kristy.

Kristy sat down next to her. "You know," she said, "when I was in fifth grade, I poured Yoo-Hoo down a boy's shirt."

Tiffany scrunched her shoulders tighter.

"Seriously," Kristy continued. "His name was Alan Gray, and he made me so mad that day. He still does. Anyway, I had done a lot of bad things that year. One time I talked back so much to my teacher, she chased me around the room. But the Yoo-Hoo episode was the last straw. I got sent home with a note."

Slowly Tiffany cast a glance over her shoulder.

"Whoa, was I scared," Kristy went on. "But I figured, hey, if I don't show my mom the note, she'll never know. So I flushed it down the toilet."

A teeny smile crept across Tiffany's face. "You did?"

"Mm-hm. I don't know why the toilet didn't clog up. Anyway, I figured my troubles were over. But they weren't. See, when my teacher didn't hear from my mom, she *called* her."

"Uh-oh," Tiffany said.

"Yeah. She asked Mom about the note, and Mom asked *me*, and . . . whew. I won't go into the gory details, but boy, did I get in trouble."

Tiffany was frowning. Kristy could tell the story had sunk in.

She didn't want to push it. "So, where's the yo-yo?"

Tiffany retrieved it from under the sofa. For the next few minutes they worked on tricks. Tiffany's mood brightened, and eventually she even started her homework — at the kitchen table.

Kristy was exhausted by the time Mr. and Mrs. Kilbourne returned. The last thing she saw before she left was Tiffany grimly reaching into her backpack and pulling out a small white envelope that was hidden in a textbook.

CHAPTER 7

GIRLS!

BE AN SMS CHEERLEADER!

ONE EMERGENCY OPENING ON THE
CHEERLEADING SQUAD!

COME TO TRYOUTS!

BRING YOUR ENERGY AND YOUR VOICE!

The sign went up Wednesday morning. Tryouts were to be in exactly two weeks minus one day.

Half of me thought it was ridiculous to even *think* of trying out. The other half thought I should at least get in shape.

We had a sub in gym that day. We could pretty much do whatever we wanted, as long as it was athletic.

Cheerleading was definitely athletic, and more interesting than volleyball. Slowly the second half of me won the cheerleading argument.

It was time for Operation Physical Fitness.

Normally I do not like gym class. Let me say that right out. Why? Because they insist on holding it in the middle of the day. You end up sweaty and gross, your hair gets all greasy, and your clothes get wrinkled in the locker. *Then* you have to go back out and face the whole school.

Honestly, it's torture.

But this was an emergency. I needed to rise to the occasion.

I tried splits. I did jumping jacks. And more splits. I thought my legs were going to fall off.

But guess what? I could do them. Splits, I mean. Not terrifically, and not superfast, but I was improving.

By the end of class, I had made my decision. I was going to try out. Two weeks was plenty of time to improve. If I didn't make it, fine. I'd feel much worse if I hadn't given it a shot.

Besides, the cheerleaders were my friends now. They'd be pulling for me. If I showed any promise at all, I probably had a good chance.

I left the gym. I was hungry. My muscles were screaming at me. But I felt great.

Luckily, my next period was lunch. I couldn't wait to feed my poor, starving, aching body. I took a salad, soup, and a cheeseburger (which is more than I usually eat) from the lunch counter, and I went right to my usual spot at the BSC table.

"Wow," said Kristy, looking at my tray.

"Is someone joining you?"

Mary Anne smiled. "Robert?"

"No," I said. "I'm just hungry."

"It's love," Claudia remarked. "They say love makes you hungrier."

"Where did you hear that?" I asked.

Claudia shrugged. "I read it somewhere. Something to do with, like, hormones or biospheres."

"Biospheres?" Kristy laughed so hard she practically spit out her food.

As I was reaching the bottom of my salad, I saw Sheila enter the cafeteria. "Hey, Sheil!" I called out.

She rushed to our table. "How's it going?" she asked.

Kristy, Mary Anne, and Claudia remained dead silent. I decided to do the only polite thing. "Have you guys all met?" I asked.

They hadn't, so I introduced everyone around. Then Sheila sat at the edge of an empty seat across from me. "Did you see our sign?"

"*I* did," Claudia piped up.

"Are any of you trying out?" Sheila said.

I could see a Look shoot around among the three of them. A you-must-be-joking Look. "I don't think so," Mary Anne answered.

"I am," I announced.

Kristy looked at me as if I'd lost my mind. But I figured, what the heck? Now that I'd made my decision, I didn't need to keep it quiet anymore.

"Great!" Sheila exclaimed, standing up from her chair. "I knew you would! Do you have a routine?"

"A routine?" I asked. "Am I supposed to have one beforehand?"

"You need one if you make it to the final cut. You know, something that's athletic but shows your dance ability, too. A lot of girls are great at splits and stuff, but they turn into clods when they try to dance. I'm sure you'll be fine. See you." She began walking to the lunch line, then turned around. "Oh, and don't forget to smile when you practice. It's good training." With her own smile, she walked away.

" 'Bye!" I called out.

I looked across the table and came face to face with the Stoneybrook Staring Squad.

I couldn't help but giggle. "What?" I said.

"You're trying out for the cheerleaders?" Kristy asked.

"Well, yeah! Is there anything wrong with that?"

"Kristy, it's not like she's joining the Marines," Claudia said. "Come on."

Kristy turned to Claudia. "I know, but I'm surprised, that's all. I mean, aren't you?"

"I guess." Claudia looked suddenly thoughtful. "Maybe Stacey's having an insulin reaction. Keep an eye on her."

"Claudia!" I said.

"Kidding!" Claudia replied with a grin. "Seriously, if that's what you want to do, it's your choice."

"I know it may sound weird," I said, "but a group of them actually approached me to tell me about the tryouts. They're really nice, you know. People have the wrong impression, just because they sit together and act like a clique. *We* sit together, and we're not so bad."

"Yeah," Kristy agreed. "But cheerleading is so . . . I don't know."

"Dumb?" I supplied.

Kristy shrugged. "I wasn't going to say it, but — "

"Well, at first *I* thought it was a dumb idea, but it kind of grew on me. The cheerleaders *do* make the basketball games more exciting."

"That's true," Kristy replied.

"*I* think it's great," Mary Anne spoke up. "I can picture you out there doing those cheers."

"Yeah, with a designer cheerleading uniform from Bloomingdale's," Claudia added.

We laughed at that.

"Can you do it and stay in the BSC?" Kristy asked.

"Practice ends at five," I said.

Kristy let out a huge sigh. "Well, in *that* case, shake those pom-poms, Stace!"

"What are you going to do about a routine?" Mary Anne asked.

"I don't know," I replied. "I guess I could make up a dance combination — "

"Ask Jessi to help you," Claudia suggested. "She'd be a great choreographer."

It was a perfect idea. And you know what? I really wanted to get the BSC involved. Maybe The Group was too cool for sleepovers, and maybe the members of the BSC were too cool for cheerleading, but they were all my friends. And who knew? Maybe they'd learn to like each other.

After lunch I saw Penny, Margie, and Corinne in the hallway. I ran to them to tell them about my decision.

Before I could open my mouth, Penny said,

75

"I heard you're trying out. That's fabulous."

"Yeah," I replied. "But I am so nervous. I've never done anything like this."

"Oh, don't worry," Margie said. "I was nervous, too. The best thing to do is just relax."

I nodded. "Uh-huh. Well, what's it going to be like? Do I just walk in and do my routine? Should I memorize one of your cheers?"

"No," Penny answered. "We'll teach everyone a cheer, very slowly. All the basic moves will be in it, so we'll be able to tell two things — how you learn, and whether or not you have the stretch and the energy and the coordination, stuff like that. If you survive the cut, you get to do the routine. We'll provide a boom box, but bring your own cassette."

"Have you started preparing a routine?" Corinne asked.

"I'm going to ask Jessi Ramsey to choreograph one with me," I replied. "She is an amazing dancer."

Corinne looked at the others. I could see the trace of a smile on her face.

Penny and Margie were smiling, too. "Uhhuh," Margie said. "Well, good luck."

"Thanks," I said. "See you!"

" 'Bye!" they replied as I turned to leave.

I tried to ignore their smiles. Corinne knew who Jessi was. She must have told the others

I hung out with sixth-graders. I guess they found that amusing.

It didn't matter. If Jessi could help me look like a good dancer, I'd be the one smiling after tryouts.

"Wow! Come on over!"

That was Jessi's reaction when I phoned to ask for her help with the routine.

"Now?" I said. "The BSC meeting starts in an hour."

"That's plenty of time!"

"Oh, okay. I'll be right there."

I clomped upstairs and changed into my Danskins. I hadn't worn them in ages. They were wrinkled and musty.

I didn't care. This week they were going to get a workout. And so was I.

I was going to blow everyone away at the tryouts.

CHAPTER 8

"Aaaaaugh! I am dying!"

My screaming did not faze Claudia one bit. She looked at the panicked face in my bedroom mirror. "What is it now, Stacey?"

I held out a fistful of my hair. "Look at this! I can't leave the house. Call Robert! Tell him to cancel!"

Claudia sighed. "Stacey, that is a hair kink. It is not the end of the world. Many girls survive on dates with a kink in their hair."

"How do you know?"

"I read a study, okay? It said that ninety-eight point two percent of all single-kink-haired girls under the age of fourteen have reported that their dates fell madly in love with them." She grabbed my brush and began running it through my hair. "It's a fact. In the Connecticut Journal of . . . Hair Disorders."

I looked at her. She looked at me.

Together we burst out laughing. I fell off my chair.

There could be only one explanation for our bizarre behavior. Fear. Absolute, sheer terror.

Friday night had come much faster than I expected. Robert was due any minute. If Claudia hadn't agreed to come over and help me out, I'd be a basket case.

I had had an awful night's sleep on Thursday, and it showed. When I awoke, my hair looked like a swamp. I showered, I brushed, I managed to get rid of the knots and twists.

But nothing could get rid of The Kink.

When I climbed back onto my chair, it had gotten worse. One whole section of my hair looked as if it were trying to rise up out of my head. "Oh, Claudia, it looks like a *wing*. Maybe I should *fly* to Robert's house and pick him up."

"Why don't you just wear a ski cap, if you're so concerned?"

"Oh, right. So I can look all flat-haired like Morticia Addams when I take it off in the theater? Puh-leeze!"

Claudia threw up her arms. "Well, at least your outfit looks good."

She was right. It did. Robert and I were only going to a movie and then a coffee shop. I didn't want to overdress but I did want to look terrific, so I decided on a pair of new jeans with a brand-new white cotton cardigan with gorgeous floral embroidery and a scalloped, crocheted neckline. On my feet were suede ankle boots. *Flat-bottomed* suede ankle boots.

"Maybe I should wear something with more of a heel," I said. "I mean, he's so *tall*, and — "

Riiiing!

I grabbed the back of the chair to keep from keeling over.

"Calm down," Claudia said. "And if you're going to fall, fall on the kink. It might straighten out."

"Claudia, don't remind me of that!" I hissed.

"*Stacey?*" Mom called from downstairs. "Robert's here!"

I gulped.

"Should I escort you by the arm?" Claudia asked.

"No, I think I can make it by myself."

Claudia followed me down the steps. In the kitchen she squeezed my hand and said, "Good luck!"

I don't remember if I answered her. As I headed for the living room, I caught a whiff of something I'd never smelled in the house.

Men's cologne. Robert was wearing cologne.

I didn't know what brand it was, but I loved it.

"Hi, Stacey!" Robert said brightly as I entered the hallway. "Wow, you look great."

"Thanks. You too!" He was wearing a zipped-up down coat, but it was nice as down coats go.

Had I noticed he had a dimple on his left cheek before? Had I noticed his eyes were so dark and deep they seemed to pull me toward him like a hidden pond on a summer evening?

Had neither Claudia nor I noticed the price tag hanging from the bottom of my cardigan?

Well, Mom did. "Oops," she said. "Let me get the scissors and cut that."

"Oh! I can't believe I left it there!" I yelped.

Robert laughed. It was a friendly laugh, not judgmental. "Don't worry. No big deal."

I could practically feel Claudia groaning in the kitchen.

Mom returned with the scissors and my coat. She cut the tag, we all said good-bye, and Robert and I left.

Mrs. Brewster was waiting in the car. "Hi, Stacey," she said, and I saw immediately where Robert got his beautiful eyes. We chatted a moment, and she asked, "Where to?"

"Well," Robert said. "I looked at the movie

listings, and . . . I don't know. What do you think?"

He handed me a carefully cut-out piece of newspaper. His mom turned on the overhead light.

I looked down the list of movies at the cineplex. *Mall Warriors II* was playing on two screens now, and the rest looked pretty boring.

"Not such a great selection," I said, giving the sheet back to him.

"Yeah." Robert stuffed it in his coat pocket. "Maybe we should just get something to eat. You know, talk, maybe take a walk. . . ."

Take a walk? In twenty-degree weather?

It sounded like a wonderful idea.

Mrs. Brewster drove us to a coffee shop called the Argo in downtown Stoneybrook. Her last words to us were, "Take your time. Call me when you're ready."

"Your mom's really nice," I said as we walked inside.

"Yeah," Robert agreed. "For a mom."

"Two?" asked a harried-looking waiter. He grabbed a couple of menus and led us to a cozy booth by a window.

As we sat, Robert asked, "Did you have dinner?"

"Yes," I replied. "But go ahead and eat, if you want. I can order a salad or something."

"I ate, too. I figured we'd be going to a movie." He scanned the menu. "These desserts look great! How about this 'Brownie Ice Cream Delight for Two'?"

"Uh, no . . ."

"Pecan pie a la mode? Or maybe carrot cake?" Suddenly he looked very solemn, as if he knew he'd made a mistake. "Or maybe something lighter, like yogurt?"

I took a deep breath. He seemed so caring and earnest. He hadn't made fun of me for being a *"girl"* on a *"diet."* Somehow I didn't feel like dancing around the truth. I'd promised myself not to say anything about my diabetes, but I thought he deserved to know.

So I told him. He listened carefully, nodding and asking questions. He didn't gag when I mentioned my injections.

And when I finished, he didn't automatically change the subject, or look at me as if I were dying. He just said, "Wow, I'm glad you told me that. Otherwise you might have felt uncomfortable."

Now, Robert could have said a lot of things. He could have told me how gorgeous I was. He could have compared my hair to a cascade of satin (well, *kinked* satin) and my eyes to sapphires.

But what he had just said was the most romantic thing I could have imagined.

I was loosening up. My hair did not bother me one bit.

"Are you ready?" The waiter was now hovering over us with pad and pen.

"Uh, a vegetable soup and a small salad," I said. "Oil and vinegar on the side."

"I'll have the double bacon cheeseburger," Robert ordered.

The waiter nodded and whisked away the menus.

"I thought you *ate*," I whispered, trying to hold back a giggle.

"I did," Robert replied. "That's why I didn't order fries."

To him, this made perfect sense.

Boys.

We talked and talked. I felt so at ease with Robert. I even found the nerve to tell him the saga of The Kink. He thought it was pretty funny. *He* was funny, too. And charming and smart — and a great listener.

I thought we'd never run out of things to say. But almost a half hour later I realized we'd missed one incredibly important topic — basketball.

I felt so rude for not bringing it up. "So," I said, "how does it feel to be on a first-place team?"

I figured he'd light up, the way RJ had when I'd mentioned basketball to him. But Robert grew very quiet and thoughtful.

"I like it," he said, nodding. "I mean, I like the *playing* part of it. I've liked basketball since I was a kid."

"Well, what other part is there?" I asked.

"You know, the status stuff."

I looked at him blankly. "Meaning what?"

He seemed disappointed in my reaction. "How can I say this. Do you know Jason Fox?" he asked.

"Yeah," I replied.

"Well, he's a very smart guy, and pretty friendly. But have you ever noticed the way he acts when he's around the team and the cheerleaders?"

I shrugged. "Kind of excited." I didn't want to say *dorky*.

"He worships us. He thinks we walk on water. Some of the guys really take advantage of him. He gives his social studies homework to a guy on our team — I won't mention any names — and the guy just copies it. You know, maybe changes a word here and there. He doesn't give Jason anything in return — but it makes Jason feel so cool. He can't wait to hand it over."

"Wow." That was an awful situation, but I wasn't sure what Robert was getting at.

"Here's another thing," he added. "I'm terrible in English. I try to read all the assignments, but nothing seems to stay in my head. Last week in class we had to write a short essay on a book, and I hadn't even read past the first chapter. I got a C on it."

"Well, that's great! You must be smarter than you think."

Robert shook his head. "All I wrote on my paper was, 'I could not finish this book.' "

"What?"

"Uh-huh. On the bottom, the teacher wrote, 'If I'd had to play Lawrenceville, I'd have the same problem. Meet me after school some day this week and we'll chat about the book.' Now, George Burke, who sits next to me, *had* read it — and loved it. He wrote on both sides of the paper. The teacher's comment was something like, 'Shows good retention but shallow understanding.' He got a C minus."

"But — that's not fair."

"I know." Robert sat back in his chair with a pained look. "It's so weird. I mean, yes, we're a good team. We'll probably win the division and all. But people treat us differently — us and the cheerleaders. Everyone's willing to bend the rules for us. Well, not *everyone*. Some teachers and students treat us like normal kids. But if I wanted to cut a class, and my English teacher knew I was in school, no problem. Some of the guys do it all the time. The girls, too."

I shook my head in disbelief. "And they all seem like such nice people."

"Sometimes they are," Robert replied. "But they can be pretty fickle, you know. That's what happens when you're used to having your way all the time. You get spoiled, then you start not thinking about other people's feelings."

"I'm glad you're not like that, Robert."

Robert began cutting his burger in half. "I'm sorry. I don't mean to be so negative."

We sat quietly for a moment, eating our food. Finally I said, "You know, I'm really glad you told me this stuff. If I become a cheerleader, I'm going to work hard not to take advantage of things."

Robert's eyes widened. *"You're* trying out?"

"Yeah. Why not?"

"Hey, that's fantastic. I hope you make it. Do the other girls know?"

"So far, Sheila, Penny, Darcy, Margie, and Corinne do."

"Uh-oh. Does Corinne know we're going out?"

My heart did a flip-flop. "Maybe. Why? Are you . . ."

Robert shook his head. "No! No. We went out once or twice. It was okay, but nothing special. Not like this."

Boy, did he know what to say to a girl.

"Anyway," he went on, "I guess *she* thought we were, you know, going steady or something. She still calls me practically every day. I don't lead her on, because I'm not that type, but I'm not mean to her either." He smiled sheepishly and shrugged. "That's Corinne."

You know what? I didn't blame Corinne at all. I had been with Robert for less than an hour, in a coffee shop with clanking plates and gruff waiters, but I was having one of the nicest nights of my life.

The only problem was, I didn't want it to end.

CHAPTER 9

Monday

This was my day at the Kilbournes. I listened to everything you said: Kristy and Shannon. I braced myself. It was kind of an anticlimax when I found out Maria wouldn't be there. But I got to know Tiffany, and I was surprised. I think she's a little different without her younger sister around....

Mary Anne went to the Kilbournes' expecting the worst. She was supposed to sit for Tiffany and Maria while Shannon and her mom went to a school concert. At the last minute, Maria had decided to go. (Shannon later told us Maria didn't care about the concert, she just wanted to get away from her sister.)

So it was Mary Anne the Meek and Tiffany the Terrible, all alone.

As the car backed out of the driveway, Mary Anne sat on the living room couch. Tiffany slumped in an armchair and stared out the window.

"Did you want to go with them, Tiffany?" Mary Anne asked.

"No way," Tiffany answered.

"Um, do you want to go outside?"

"No!"

"Okay. I was just asking. I noticed you were looking outside."

"Mm."

Mary Anne quietly opened her backpack and took out some schoolbooks. She decided to use her sullen-child strategy. She wouldn't try to make Tiffany laugh or do anything. Mary Anne would just be *there*. She would be all ears if Tiffany decided she needed someone.

For a long time, Tiffany just moped around.

90

Mary Anne heard her run up and down the stairs, then open the kitchen cabinets a few times.

Finally Tiffany came into the living room and sat down on the floor. "I'm bored," she announced.

Mary Anne closed her book. "Oh?"

"Yeah. There's nothing to do. And you are the most boringest baby-sitter I've ever met."

I told you Mary Anne is extremely sensitive. But she's also an incredible baby-sitter. She knew not to take it personally. "I thought you wanted to be left alone," she said.

"I did. But I guess I don't anymore."

"Good. What do you want to do?"

"I don't know. *You're* the baby-sitter. You're supposed to find things for me to do."

"I'd be happy to, but you have to tell me what you like. How about board games?"

"Yuck."

"Do you like art?"

"Double yuck!"

"Well, you must like *something*."

Tiffany didn't answer. She looked sort of hurt and distracted.

Mary Anne sighed. "Tiffany, is something bothering you?"

Tiffany's head slumped forward. Her hair fell in front of her face. "I guess," she muttered.

"You look sad," Mary Anne said.

For a long moment Tiffany said nothing. When she finally did speak, her voice was practically a whisper. "I can't do art. I can't do board games. I can't do *anything*."

"Sure you can," Mary Anne reassured her. "Kristy mentioned you had a yo-yo — "

"It was Kristy's yo-yo," Tiffany replied. "And I couldn't even do that. I just watched. I'm so uncoordinated."

Mary Anne reached out to her. "I'm sure you're not."

Tiffany lurched up and walked to the window. "I *am*. Uncoordinated and stupid. I don't know how to swim, I'm not good in school, I can't speak any languages — "

"Those are all things your sisters do."

"I know!"

"Well, sisters are different from each other — different interests, different abilities. Just like other people. There's nothing wrong with that."

"Yeah, except my sisters have *all* the interests and abilities, and I don't have any. Shannon's a genius. She knows everything. She has so many awards, she can't even find some of them! All the teachers talk about her. It's 'Shannon this' and 'Shannon that.' Then they expect me to be the same way, and they always get so disappointed. And now Maria's bringing home all these dumb trophies. I'm like a freak in this family. I *never* win awards."

Mary Anne's heart went out to Tiffany. "You sound like you feel pretty lonely."

Tiffany's lower lip quivered. Her eyes filled. "You know, Maria and I used to do stuff together all the time. I guess because Shannon's so much older, and always so busy. So we kind of stuck together. But now Maria's just as bad."

Mary Anne thought for a moment. Tiffany needed something to take her mind off her sisters. "You know what?" she said finally. "You need a hobby."

"Huh?"

"An interest of your own. Something your sisters don't necessarily do. I mean, Shannon has school, Maria has swimming — and now we have to find something for Tiffany."

Tiffany looked doubtful. "Like what?"

"That's for you to decide. I can help you make a list." Mary Anne pulled a notebook and pen out of her shoulder bag. "Say anything that pops into your mind."

"What are the most popular hobbies?"

"I guess drawing, painting, music, dance. . . ."

Tiffany hopped onto the couch. "Okay. Those are good. Also, I have a friend who has about a million plants and flowers. And another who collects stamps. And Wendy Kasser plays the piano."

"Whoa, slow down." Mary Anne carefully wrote down the three suggestions, then offered, "There's also tennis and bird-watching."

"Surfing!"

"Uh, maybe not this time of year. How about snow sculptures?"

The ideas kept coming. When the list grew to both sides of the page, they stopped. Tiffany held it up excitedly and said, "I'm going to start trying some right now!"

She ran through the kitchen and down to the basement. Mary Anne heard her clanking around for a few minutes.

Tiffany came upstairs with an old tennis racket, a book on photography, a blank photo album, a jigsaw puzzle, and a ratty old piano instruction book called *Teaching Little Fingers to Play*. She plopped everything on the living room floor.

"Wow!" Mary Anne said. She could hardly believe the change.

"I know I'll find a hobby I can beat Shannon and Maria with," Tiffany squealed. "And there's so much more stuff down there. Mary Anne, this was the *best* idea."

She ran out of the living room again.

Mary Anne settled back and pulled out some homework from her bag. She was thrilled. Tiffany would be occupied for awhile. More important, she was happy.

That was a major triumph.

CHAPTER 10

"Okay, let's try it again," Jessi commanded. "*Chassé* left, *chassé* right, step, *kick*, step, *kick*. *Don't* forget your *arms*, Stacey — *el*bows straight *up*, that's it, now *turn*, turn, *pump* those arms, jump . . . jump . . . *split!*"

I sank to the ground with a gasp. I clutched the ground for support. My right leg was bent at the knee. My hair was hanging in front of my face. The only thing I could say was, "Ugh."

It was Tuesday, one week from tryouts. I'd been practicing with Jessi every day. She had worked out a routine that looked spectacular when she demonstrated it.

The only problem was, she wasn't the one trying out. I was.

And I still wasn't getting it.

"That was almost perfect!" Jessi exclaimed. "Except for the final tableau. Remember, it's like this."

She sank into a perfect split, reaching to the sky, her head tilted back with a great big smile.

I swear that girl must have rubber bands instead of bones.

"How do you do that?" I asked.

"The same way you do!" she replied. "Stacey, you look good, I promise. You're just thinking too much about the routine. Don't worry, you *know* it. Just trust your body — and smile!"

"Right." I smiled. My left leg barked at me. (Well, that's what it *felt* like.)

I was having second thoughts about trying out. (Can you tell?)

We worked and worked until I was ready to collapse. Needless to say, that night I slept like a rock.

The next morning, Wednesday, I literally fell out of bed. My legs did not want to uncurl. I sprawled on the floor and did long, slow, stretching exercises, just the way Jessi had taught me. After a few minutes of that, I was ready for the school day.

Believe it or not, as I walked to school I felt better than I had for a few days. Over the weekend my legs had been like Jell-O. Now they felt stronger and more solid.

Guess who was in front of school as I arrived? Robert and Marty.

They were deep in conversation, but I caught Robert's eye.

He stopped in midsentence. "Hi, Stacey!" he said.

"Hey, Stace," Marty echoed. With a mischievous smile, he added, "Well, I guess I should leave you guys alone. See you!"

He loped away from the school with long, gliding steps.

"Where's he going?" I asked.

"Emergency basketball drill," Robert replied in a flat voice.

"What?"

"Well, that was what he told his homeroom teacher, Mr. Blake." Robert shrugged. "Blake's a big fan, so he lets Marty go."

"But that's not fair."

"Yeah, I know. That's what I was trying to tell Marty."

I was shocked. But it made me think of the time Penny and Darcy had met me outside my homeroom. They had giggled about going to a "practice."

Sheila hadn't gone with them. Ms. Levine would never have fallen for that excuse. Obviously Penny and Darcy were luckier.

"I can't believe teachers let stuff like this happen," I said.

"Mm-hm. It's as much their fault as the kids'." Robert sighed and put his arm around me. "But don't worry. Some of us are okay."

I supposed so, but I felt pretty funny about the situation. Robert had told me this kind of stuff happened. Still, seeing it was creepy.

Robert walked me to my locker. There we met Mary Anne and Logan.

"Hey, we were just talking about you," Logan exclaimed.

"Yeah?" Robert replied.

"We're going out Saturday night," Mary Anne said. "And we thought you might want to make it a double date."

I thought it was a great idea. But Robert looked a little disappointed. "Well, I was going to ask Stacey to go out with me on Friday."

"You were?" I asked.

Robert nodded. "Is it okay with you if we go out two nights in a row?"

"Yes!" I blurted out. "I accept and I accept!"

Boy, was I psyched. That evening before the BSC meeting, I really threw myself into my cheerleading practice.

That was when I had a breakthrough. I don't know how it happened. Everything just seemed to click. My kicks were sharp, my steps were on the beat, my arms were energetic. I even managed to smile through most of the routine.

"Stacey, you are going to blow their socks

off!" Jessi said. "I am serious. Socks will be flying all around you. The cheerleaders'll be running around in their bare feet. That was fantastic!"

"We're the best! Stace and Jess! Yea, team!" I shouted. I was fired up. For the first time, I knew I had a shot at making the team.

"You should preview this at the BSC meeting," Jessi suggested.

"Are you kidding?"

"No way. Aren't you proud of it?"

"Well, yeah, but . . ."

"It'll be like a dress rehearsal. If you can do it well before them, you'll be *great* at the tryouts."

"Maybe."

"I knew you would!" Jessi exclaimed.

"I said *maybe*."

You know, sometimes I think Jessi is just as bad as Kristy. That evening, at "new business" time in the meeting, Jessi stood up and said, "I move we all go into the Kishis' backyard at six and watch Stacey's cheerleading routine!"

Claudia cracked up. She thought it was a joke. And Kristy got impatient. But Jessi insisted — and that was how I got my first audience. At precisely six, my friends and I ran out to the backyard. I was on.

How did I do? Not bad, considering I was wearing my down coat and snow boots. Kristy and Claudia still seemed to think I was crazy, but they applauded.

Good old Mary Anne said, "Stacey, that was great! If you were a cheerleader I wouldn't be able to watch the game!"

Now *that* is a friend.

On Thursday I had my second dress rehearsal. This one was planned. I couldn't help blabbing to Sheila about my progress, and I asked her if she and a couple of the others would watch my routine in advance.

I went with her to The Group table during lunch period. She whispered to Penny and Darcy, and the four of us headed for the rear door, which led to the school parking lot.

"We can't go out there," I said. "We'll get suspended."

Penny laughed. "Don't worry."

This teacher, Mr. Schubert, was standing near the door. He began staring at us. Darcy just smiled at him and called out, "Just a little drill review. We'll be back in two minutes."

Mr. Schubert nodded.

I felt a little nervous about breaking the rules, even though Mr. Schubert had okayed it, so I ran through the routine quickly. By that time I was pretty confident, and I don't think I made any mistakes.

The girls' eyes were wide when I finished.

They looked totally surprised. I wasn't sure whether I'd been better or worse than they had expected.

"Did you like it?" I asked.

Penny nodded. *"Yeah."*

"Any suggestions?"

They shook their heads. "Just do exactly what you did," Sheila said. "You are good, Stacey. *Really* good."

Well, I was as high as a kite. But I didn't want to assume I'd get in. I practiced really hard Thursday evening, and then again on Friday after school.

Friday night was my dinner date with Robert. He knew I needed to eat right after the BSC meeting, so you know what he did? He decided to surprise me outside the Kishis' at six.

As we barreled out of the house, Jessi was the first to see him. She stopped in her tracks and gasped, "Oh, wow! Is this him?"

Robert blushed, and we all cracked up. (Jessi, by the way, was mortified. She didn't stop apologizing to me for a week.) By this time, the other members of the BSC, except for Shannon, had already met Robert. He'd sat at the BSC table in the cafeteria a couple of times.

Needless to say, every one of them liked him. (How could they not?)

Well, my weekend was off to a perfect start. We ate dinner at Robert's house, and then his dad drove us to a rock concert in Stamford. That was where I learned, in the aisle of Row 34, that Robert was a very cool dancer.

The next day, Saturday, SMS had an afternoon game (which, of course, we won). Watching the cheerleaders, I felt great. I could do everything they could. Watching Robert, I felt even better. One time he actually winked at me from the court.

Our double date with Logan and Mary Anne that night was hysterical. We went bowling, and the only one who was able to roll the ball straight was . . . Mary Anne! It seemed to take years for her ball to reach the pins, but she always managed to knock some down. Logan looked a little upset by this, but Robert thought it was great. He called Mary Anne a natural athlete. He even invited her to try out for the basketball team. We went out for ice cream afterward (I ordered nachos). To tell you the truth, I don't know how we were able to get any food in our mouths. We hardly stopped laughing.

Sunday was another practice day. Jessi came over for a final tuneup. We added a few new flourishes to the routine. I made sure Jessi pointed out even my slightest mistakes.

By the end of the session, I felt that I could do the routine in my sleep. My splits felt fabulous. My arms were strong. A smile never left my face.

I was ready.

CHAPTER 11

"Breathe, Stacey. Just breathe."

Jessi's arm was around my shoulder. My knees were knocking against each other. The noise around me was deafening.

On the gym floor, dozens of girls were doing last-minute practicing. The bleachers in the SMS gym were chock full of boyfriends, girlfriends, and siblings. It looked as if half the female student body had shown up for tryouts. I didn't even recognize some of the faces.

Tuesday had snuck up on me. I spent all weekend and all Monday impatiently waiting — but now that it was here, I was petrified.

Kristy, Mary Anne, Claudia, Shannon, and Mallory were sitting around me in the bleachers, like a wall of protection. (Yes, *Mallory*, who was getting over mono! She said she wouldn't miss it for the world.) Behind them were Logan and Robert.

The BSC had pulled together to support me, despite the fact that most of them didn't care much for The Group. We went over my routine move by move at the Monday meeting. We almost had to cut the meeting short because Kristy accidentally kicked the phone out of the wall during a cartwheel demonstration.

Now my friends had become my personal cheering squad. I couldn't let them down.

I looked at the gym clock. Three forty-one. Four minutes to go. I tried to run through the combination in my head.

Bad idea.

"Jessi, what comes after chassé *right?"* I cried.

Jessi rolled her eyes. *"Chassé* left. Now stop it, Stacey. Don't overthink."

"Sing a song to yourself," Mary Anne suggested.

"Relax," Claudia said.

"Do some wind sprints," was Kristy's advice.

Stop thinking, sing, relax, and sprint.

Right. No problem.

Phwweeeeet!

A loud whistle made the gym go silent. I could hear Darcy's voice call out, "Girls, please clear the floor and be quiet! We have to begin!"

Everyone scampered into the bleachers. The cheerleaders themselves were in front row center, sitting behind a big folding table. They were dressed in their SMS outfits, and each of them held a clipboard. Sheila's hair was pulled back, and she looked like a movie star. Darcy and Corinne had tucked pencils neatly behind their ears. Penny and Margie were giggling about something with a couple of the girls I didn't know.

They all looked so breezy and confident. I would have given anything to switch places with them.

"All right, listen up!" Darcy shouted. "This is a much bigger group than we expected. We don't want this to drag on until night, so we have to move fast. First you're all going to learn a simple combination. We'll circulate among you and let you know who makes the final cut. Whoever's left gets to show us your own routine."

A girl in the back of the bleachers shouted, "You mean, if you cut us we won't be able to do the routine we prepared?"

Darcy gave her an icy look. "Uh, yes, that's what I said. Now come on, let's line up!"

The girls began running down the bleachers. They sounded like a herd of elephants.

Elephants, however, would never dream of dressing the way some of these girls did. Neon-pattern aerobic suits, French-cut leotards, expensive-looking shorts with button shirts tied at the waist. I was in the middle of a fashion show.

"Go ahead, Stacey!" Jessi whispered.

I stood up to a chorus of "Good luck!" from my friends. I adjusted my Danskin outfit and walked to the gym floor.

A logjam had formed in front of the cheerleaders. Everyone wanted to be in the front row. Girls were standing so close together, they would have knocked each other out if they had had to do a kick.

I guess that would have been one way of making the first cut.

"Whoa, stop it!" Darcy shouted. "Let's spread out! You're all going to get an equal chance!"

The cheerleaders plunged into the crowd, gently pushing and pulling the girls farther into the gym. It made me think of cattle rustling.

When we were finally spread out, the cheerleaders distributed themselves around the gym. Darcy announced, "Okay, make sure you can see one of us. We'll demonstrate the routine twice, and you join in the third time."

I was on the left side of the group, at about the middle of the gym. Sheila had made sure to be the cheerleader nearest me. She saw me over her shoulder and gave a smile.

Darcy pressed a button on a boom box in the bleachers. A rock song blared through the gym.

Well, the combination they did was embarrassingly easy. A few simple steps, kicks, and turns, and one split at the end.

Everyone would be able to do it, I thought. It would be impossible for them to cut anybody.

I was wrong. You'd think some of those girls had never learned their right from their left. And their faces! Half of them looked as if they were being tortured. Not to mention the "cheer," which sounded like a chain gang chant.

"You must be kidding!" Darcy's voice boomed out. "Come on! Have some *fun* with this!"

After running through the routine a few more times, the cheerleaders began walking around the room. They would casually look over the crowd, then whisper into the ear of a girl.

I was one of the first who got a whisper. It was Sheila, saying, "Get away from these goons. We want to see your routine."

I walked to the stands. My BSC friends were staring at me, all confused. "You got *cut*?" Jessi exclaimed.

"I got kept," I said, "for the finals."

They jumped up and cheered. We waited patiently until only the finalists (and their friends) were left in the stands — twelve finalists altogether.

In the back of the gym, near the locker room door, the rejected girls were murmuring and complaining. Some were sobbing. The one who had asked the question earlier was at the table in front, pleading with Darcy.

Before long that girl was running for the locker room door, weeping uncontrollably. Darcy just looked annoyed.

"Okay," she announced. "I'm going to assign you each a number. Remember it, because that's the order of your routine."

She pointed to us, one by one, counting out numbers. I was five.

The torture began. Number One was Kathleen Lopez — tall, willowy-thin like a model, and stunning. She even looked great giving her cassette to Darcy. Her routine was pretty good, too. I was dying. "Jessi . . ." I moaned.

"No comparison," Jessi whispered. "Not even close."

Lisa Kedem, Ronnie Gallea, and Diane Magnani followed. Each of them had a decent routine — but none of them had been trained by the great Jessi Ramsey, and it showed.

I was beginning to calm down.

"Number Five!" Darcy shouted. "Who's Number — "

"Here!" I said, jumping up.

From behind me, I heard: "Go!" "Good luck!" "Break a leg!" "Show 'em!"

Jessi and I shared a Look. Now she seemed more nervous than I did.

I took my cassette and walked to Darcy, flashing my biggest, happy-to-be-here smile.

What happened next? It's all a blur. My body was on auto-pilot. Here's what I remember: I kept smiling. I didn't lose my place. And the cheerleaders did not take their eyes off me during my performance.

When I was done, my BSC friends gave me a loud standing ovation.

I stood up, panting and sweaty. My breathing sounded like a hacksaw in the vast gym. Very chic.

I couldn't help staring at the cheerleaders. I knew they couldn't tell me on the spot whether I'd be chosen, but I wanted to see something — a signal, a facial expression.

They were all huddled over their clipboards, writing furiously. But as I began walking back to the stands, Sheila looked up and gave me a confident nod.

My friends were still standing. "You were *sensational!*" Shannon said.

"Definitely the best!" Kristy cried.

"Sssshhhhh, Kristy, not so loud!" Mary Anne warned. "Be polite."

"She's right, though," Robert said in a softer voice. "Far and away the best!"

Jessi was beaming with pride. "I agree. I am *sooo* proud of you!"

We stayed to watch the others. After tryouts were finally over, Darcy turned and said, "Thank you for coming. You were all fantastic. We'll make our decision by Friday, and it's going to be a hard one. See you then."

The twelve girls and their friends cheered wildly. I'm sure the other finalists felt just as relieved as I did.

As we stood to leave, Jessi leaned forward and whispered in my ear. "You know what? You're a shoo-in."

My friends nodded.

"Really?" I replied. "You're not just being polite?"

"No way," Jessi said. "Cross my heart."

"Stace," Robert added, putting his arm around me, "you were a nine-one-one."

I glanced at the cheerleader table. The girls were in furious conversation, but Sheila was looking right at me. She grinned from ear to ear and gave me a thumbs-up sign.

I nearly shrieked.

CHAPTER 12

Wednesday

Today was my turn with Tifany. I was
kind of looking forward to it, after what
mary ann wrote about her wanting to
learn hobies. I was hopping Tifany might
want to do some art stuff

Well, I dont knoe if you realise it,
Mary anne, but you really opened up
a can of werms....

Claudia was on a mission To Create An Artist. She had done it once before, with a sitting charge named Rosie Wilder. Rosie had a million talents but was unhappy, and Claudia helped her realize she loved art more than anything else.

Tiffany was going to be Claud's next project.

Claud arrived at the Kilbournes' energetic and happy. Shannon was at some meeting, as usual. Mrs. Kilbourne and Maria were rushing off to a swim meet.

"Tiffany's in the rec room!" was the last thing Mrs. Kilbourne said. "Enter at your own risk! 'Bye!"

Claudia cheerfully walked to the rec room and pushed the door open. "Hi, Ti — "

Bonk. The door hit something and went no further.

"Hey, quit it!" a voice shouted.

Claudia peeked through the crack in the door. "It's Claudia, your — "

Two tries, two unfinished sentences. Claudia could only stare.

She had never seen such a mess — *Claudia*, the winner of the Least Likely to See Her Own Bedroom Floor Award.

Photo albums and a camera were stacked on the TV set. A tennis racket, baseball glove, and softball lay on the couch, next to a cassette recorder and about a dozen tapes. The floor was covered with jigsaw puzzle pieces, stamps, an old guitar, Polaroid pictures, photography magazines, coins, lumps of modeling clay, paste, glue, paints, chalk, plastic containers, a model-making kit, and books about horses, birds, jogging, sculpting, music, and space travel.

Tiffany stood up and waded through the junk. She pulled a huge easel away from the door and said, "Okay, come in."

Claudia took a couple of steps in, but that was as far as she could go. "Uh . . . what are you doing?"

"Lots of things," Tiffany replied.

"Are these all . . . *hobbies*?" Claudia asked.

Tiffany whirled around and gave her an accusing look. "Who told you?"

"What?"

"Who *told* you? Did Mary Anne tell you I was looking for a hobby?"

"Well, yeah. Was it supposed to be a secret?"

Tiffany pushed aside the tennis racket and plopped onto the couch. "I guess not." She let out a huge sigh. "Do you have a hobby?"

"Uh-huh. Art. Can I sit next to you?"

"Yeah." Tiffany put the cassette player on the floor and Claudia sat down. "Music is easy to listen to," Tiffany went on, "but it's real hard to play. I tried playing the guitar. I even read a book about it. But when I played I sounded like a dying cat."

"When I sing, I sound like a howling dog," Claudia said. "Maybe we could do a duet."

Tiffany smiled. "What kind of art do you do?"

"Painting, sculpture, drawing, everything."

"Well, I tried everything."

"You couldn't have given it much of a chance, Tiffany — "

"I *did*. But I stink. Also I didn't like it. It's too messy."

"What did you like?"

"*Nothing!* I try to hit a tennis ball against the garage door, and I miss half the time. When I take pictures, I cut people's heads off. Jigsaw puzzles are boring. Birds all look the same to me, and so do horses. Besides I've seen them and they're smelly. We don't have a piano. And I get sick licking stamps."

"Uh, Tiffany, maybe you should think of going a little slower, picking one thing — "

"I *can't!*" Tiffany got up from the sofa. She began stalking around the room, kicking things aside. "I can tell when I'm bad at something. I have to find a hobby I can *win* at."

"Win? Who are you trying to beat?"

"My sisters! Didn't Mary Anne tell you *that*?

That's why I'm doing this. Mary Anne told me to."

"Wait a minute," Claudia said. "I don't think Mary Anne meant that you should try to compete with your sisters."

"She did! Ask her! We can call her up — "

"No, that's okay. Look, Tiffany, this isn't making you happy, is it?"

Tiffany moped over to the couch again and sank into the cushion. "No."

"I think you may be doing this the wrong way. I mean, a hobby is something you should *enjoy*. It doesn't matter how good you are at it. It's not supposed to be, like, a *weapon* against your sisters."

Tiffany mumbled something.

"You know," Claudia continued, "my older sister, Janine, is so smart it's disgusting."

"Shannon is like that!"

"Well, I felt so inferior to Janine that I used to escape to my room all the time and just draw pictures. It made me forget how stupid I felt. Then I got into painting, and papier-mâché, jewelry-making. Now I've become pretty good at all of it, and I want to be an artist for a living someday. I didn't try to be better than my sister. I stuck to the thing I liked."

Tiffany looked deep in thought. (Either that

or bored out of her mind. Claudia wasn't sure which.)

"Tiffany," Claudia said, "what do you like? What really interests you? Come on, first thing that comes to your mind."

For a moment, Tiffany said nothing. Then she looked up at Claudia and said in a tiny voice, "Flowers."

"Flowers?"

"I guess."

"You like looking at them?"

Tiffany's face lost all its gloominess. "I like *everything* about them — planting, watering, watching them grow, arranging them, and drying the petals to make sachets."

It wasn't what Claudia had expected. But boy, was she glad to see Tiffany excited about *something*.

"That's a great hobby, Tiffany!" Claudia said. "Maybe your parents can let you grow a garden in the spring. I mean, there's not much you can do now, but — "

"Sure there is, silly!" Tiffany bolted from the couch and ran out of the room, slipping over all her junk. Moments later she returned with a stack of magazines and an encyclopedia. "We get *House and Garden*. I always look at the pictures when Mom and Dad are through. See, I can use these pictures to *plan* my garden. Then I can look up the plants and flowers I

118

don't know in the encyclopedia."

"How about mapping it out on paper?" Claudia asked.

Tiffany squealed with delight. "Ooh, then I can draw it with colored pencils!"

She ran off again, this time returning with pencils and huge sheets of paper.

Claudia said Tiffany worked on her garden plan the rest of the afternoon. When Mrs. Kilbourne came home she couldn't believe the change. She offered to adopt Claudia (jokingly, I think).

As Claudia left, she could see Tiffany and Maria staking out a corner of the backyard. They were gesturing at the dirt and talking a mile a minute.

CHAPTER 13

I don't know how I kept food down. But there I was, in the SMS cafeteria on Thursday, somehow eating a Salisbury steak. (I wish someone would tell me why they call a hamburger with old brown sauce "Salisbury steak." Did someone named Salisbury invent the sauce? If so, he should have been arrested.)

My eyes kept darting over to The Group's table. They were jabbering away about something. Jason Fox was standing next to them, probably giving Marty some homework answers.

I looked away. Seeing them only made me feel worse.

The tryouts had been held two days earlier. Results weren't going to be announced until the next day. I had to walk the same halls as the cheerleaders, go to some of the same classes, eat the same Salisbury steak.

Nervous? Me? Why do you ask?

I tried to analyze Sheila's tone of voice when she said "Good morning" in homeroom. When Penny smiled at me in the hallway, I was convinced I was going to make the squad. When Darcy seemed hassled after school I was sure I'd been rejected.

Robert was being awfully nice to me. He tried to make me laugh, which always helped — briefly.

My concentration was shot. Three huge pimples had burst onto my face. My stomach was making noises loud enough to stop conversations.

And the worst thing was, *everyone else was so calm!*

"Shannon told me Tiffany wants to plant ivy along the side of the house," Claudia was saying. "She even knows the *kind.* Her mom thinks it's okay, but her dad says it'll weaken the walls."

Tiffany was the hot topic at lunch. Shannon had called Claudia Wednesday night, marveling at the change in her sister.

Bits of Claudia's conversation were breaking through the mush in my brain. One thing stuck with me, though. Something about choosing a hobby for the right reason. It made such good sense. I don't know if I would have thought to tell that to Tiffany.

"Stacey? Are you okay?" Mary Anne asked.

I nodded. "Yeah. I'm just thinking about . . . you know."

"Hey, don't worry," Kristy said. "Just try to forget about it."

"That's easy for you to say," I replied.

Mmmmmmrrraawwww. . . .

I had never heard a sound like that escape from my belly. It was like a yawning lion. Maybe the Salisbury steak had woken it up.

"That's easy for *you* to say," Kristy remarked.

Suddenly I wasn't feeling very well. "Um . . . I'm going to go to the girls' room," I said.

Suddenly my friends looked tense and concerned. "Do you need help?" Claudia asked.

I knew what they were thinking. "It's not the diabetes. Just an upset stomach."

I grabbed my shoulder bag and stood up. The girls' room was across the hall. I rushed inside and closed myself in a stall. I *hate hate hate HATE* barfing, but I'd rather do it in private if I have to.

I took a few deep breaths. My stomach seemed to be settling. The lion must have shifted and gone back to sleep. I promised myself not to eat any more lunch.

That was when I heard the bathroom door slam open. "Aaagh! I can't *believe* you kissed him, right in front of everybody!"

It was Penny's voice. Laughter bounced off the tile walls. She was with a few other cheerleaders.

The lion stirred.

"Did you see the lipstick on his cheek?" Margie cried.

"No," Darcy replied, "because his face turned the same color!"

More laughter. Corinne's voice chanted, "Margie and Jason, Margie and Jason . . ."

"Oh, for *sure*, Corinne," Margie said. "Every *day*."

I was petrified. I wanted to leave the stall, but I must have looked terrible. Quickly I pulled a comb out of my shoulder bag. I let out a silent burp, which made me feel much better.

Outside the stall I could hear purses opening and makeup clattering. The girls were now standing by the sinks, presumably looking in the mirrors.

I prepared myself for my entrance.

"I can't wait for this tryout meeting to be over," Penny said.

"Really!" Margie exclaimed. "I *hate* having to face those girls in the hallway. Did you see Stacey today?"

"The poor thing looked like she was going to faint," Darcy said.

My hand froze on the latch. Should I burst

in on a conversation about me? How embarrassing! But if I stayed where I was, and they found out I'd been there, they'd know I'd been eavesdropping. I wasn't sure what to do.

"Well, I don't know why she's going mental about it," Margie said. "She did great."

"Yeah," Penny agreed.

I decided to postpone my entrance.

"Where did she *learn* all that stuff?" Penny asked.

"From the Baby-sitters Club," Corinne answered.

The rest of the girls burst out laughing.

"Don't be nasty, Corinne," Margie scolded.

"I know what you mean, though," Penny said in a condescending voice. "She does hang around them all the time."

"No, seriously," Corinne insisted. "She learned the dance routine from that sixth-grader she hangs around with. Remember — Jessi?"

"From Jessi?" Penny said. "No way. She's too young. Where could *she* have learned to dance like that? *Sesame Street*?"

"Well, wherever Stacey learned it," Margie replied, "she sure can move. And she's pretty and smart. Plus she's got a strong voice."

"*I* think she'd be a great cheerleader," Margie said.

"Yeah," Penny agreed.

"Uh-huh," Darcy murmured. "Better than *you*."

"Stop," Penny protested.

"I hate to say it," Margie chimed in, "but she's better than all of us."

I thought I was going to scream with joy. I could just picture myself in a cheerleader outfit. I squeezed the toilet paper roll with all my might to keep from bursting.

"She seems pretty nice," Darcy remarked. "Do you guys know her well?"

"Sheila knows her best," Penny replied. "She likes her."

"So does Robert," Margie added.

"Is *she* lucky," Darcy said.

Corinne exhaled loudly. "You guys, don't get me started. You're doing this on purpose."

"Oh, *please*, Corinne," Darcy replied.

"Here we go again," muttered Margie.

"You are *so* insensitive!" Corinne complained. "I have feelings, you know. And I've got news for you. If it weren't for Little Miss *Baby*-sitter, Robert and I would still be going out. She had to come along with her bouncy-bouncy hair, and now I've lost him!"

Penny laughed. "Corinne, you never *had* him!"

"Shows how much *you* know!" Corinne shot back.

"Uh, can we change the subject, please?"

Darcy said. "Save the fighting for after school, hmmm?"

Clatter, clatter, clickety-click went the makeup kits as the room quieted down.

Bouncy-bouncy hair? I had never heard that one. The nerve!

Soon the girls began talking again. The topic switched from makeup to clothes to the members of the basketball team.

I listened with half an ear. Despite what Corinne had said about me, I couldn't help but feel excited. The girls liked my routine. They said I'd be a good cheerleader. I heard it with my own ears.

I sat tight, struggling to keep my excitement in. I waited for the girls to leave, counted to a hundred, and opened the stall door.

When I walked out of the girls' room, I wore a huge smile on my face. My hair was bouncing, and I was glad. My stomach was as calm as could be.

CHAPTER 14

"*Attention, please. Will all girls who made the final callback for the cheerleading squad please meet at the gym at the beginning of eighth-grade lunch period.*"

The announcement came at the end of homeroom on Friday. I had to grab my desk. I thought I'd melt and slide to the floor.

I didn't dare look back at Sheila. We had agreed early in the week not to talk about the tryouts. I didn't want to spend the morning analyzing whatever facial expression I'd see if I turned around.

When the bell rang, I headed straight for the door.

I met Robert in the hallway on the way to my first-period class. "Good luck, Stacey," he said, "but I'm sure you don't need it."

My hands were shaking. "I don't know how I'll last till lunch."

Robert smiled and pulled out an envelope

that was tucked into a book. "Here, maybe this will help."

I took the envelope and opened it. Inside was a card with a photo of a girl in a cheerleading outfit. She was at the top of a jump, looking downward. Her eyes were buggy with shock. Clouds surrounded her, and a bird was flying by with a thought bubble that showed a question mark.

Two words were printed inside: HIGH THERE. Underneath, Robert had written, *To my favorite cheerleader. You're great.*

Robert's face was turning red. "Corny, I know, but — "

"No, it's *sweet*, Robert," I said. "I love it."

"I was going to give it to you afterward, but you looked like you could use a boost now."

"Thank you!" I threw my arms around him.

Robert walked me to my class. He was right. The card had given me a boost. He was obviously confident about the outcome of the tryouts. *Everyone* was.

My own confidence kept leaving me every few minutes. During my morning classes, I had to *will* parts of my body to stop shaking. Twice my teachers asked if I was having a diabetic reaction.

By the time lunch period finally came, I must have aged about ten years. I felt numb.

Slowly I walked to the gym. I hoped the

beating of my heart wasn't too obvious under my blouse.

I took a seat in the bleachers. Several of the other girls were there. We sat near each other, but no one said a word.

The cheerleaders were milling around, swapping clipboards, laughing and gossiping. They looked relieved. Fortunately Sheila's back was to me every time I looked her way. I didn't want to see her until the announcement was over.

"Okay, is everybody here?" Darcy called out. She approached us, counting heads. "I guess so. Okay, we can start."

With a solemn expression, she began slowly pacing. The other cheerleaders sat in the first row. "First off," Darcy said, "I want to say you were all wonderful. If we had twelve spots, we would have taken you all. We thought this was the best group yet."

The other cheerleaders nodded and mumbled enthusiastically.

"Now, unfortunately, we have to face the facts. Eleven of you will not make it. All that means is that you're in good company. Our decision was based on many things — talent and looks, of course; but also personality, height, physique, and ability to fit with the existing squad."

Puh-leeze! This was *torture*. Where did she

think she was, the Miss America Pageant? Couldn't she just come out with it?

"We feel like we've gotten to know you, and we want you to keep in touch. After all, next year at SHS, we'll be in the same boat, trying out together!"

Polite, nervous laughter from the girls around me.

"All right, now. After a long, long night, staying up and discussing every detail of every performance, going back and forth between all our excellent choices, we finally made our decision. I know you're dying to know, so here it is. The new member of the SMS cheerleading squad is . . ."

She paused. I felt as if electricity were crackling through me.

". . . Kathleen Lopez!"

My legs had been poised to stand. They seemed to be saying to the rest of my body, *Come on, we can't stay like this forever.* It took awhile for my shocked brain to send the bad news downward.

On the gym floor, the cheerleaders were hugging and congratulating Kathleen.

Kathleen Lopez?

Her routine flashed through my mind — her decent but not spectacular turns, her okay split, her nice but wavering smile.

I tried to live with the decision. I didn't want to be a sore loser. It was over. The best girl won. I stood up and got ready to leave.

But the moment my foot touched the floor, I stopped. Who was I trying to kid? Kathleen's routine had *not* been as good as mine. I wasn't being conceited, it was just true.

All kinds of thoughts were whisking around in my brain. Robert's comments about the way The Group manipulated people, about their fickleness. The remarks I'd overheard in the bathroom about me. About Jessi. About Corinne.

Corinne! Could she have convinced them not to take me?

My blood was boiling. I walked right up to the happy group. Margie was the nearest girl. I tapped her on the shoulder.

She turned around. Her smile tightened. "Hi, Stacey."

"Margie, why didn't I make the squad?" I said it flat out. I was not going to pull any punches.

"Well . . . it was a hard decision, and . . ." She shrugged. "We just, you know, picked the best girl."

She gave me this condescending, *nothing-more-I-can-do* look, then turned around again.

It wasn't true. Something else had hap-

131

pened. I have pretty good instincts, and they were screaming foul right now. I felt like grabbing Margie by that shoulder. I felt like crying. I felt like screaming. I could barely see straight.

When my eyes cleared, I caught a glimpse of Corinne. She was backing away from the others and signaling me to follow.

She led me to a secluded corner of the gym.

I didn't know how to read her face. She wore a sympathetic expression, but I couldn't tell if she was just arranging her features that way. I didn't trust anybody at that point.

"Stacey, I know how you must feel," she said.

I bit my lip.

"But I have to tell you the truth. Kathleen wasn't better than you. We all knew that."

I could feel my mouth drop open. "Then what happened?"

"You're not going to like this, Stacey." She sighed. "The reason you didn't make it was because you were *too* good. You're *so* talented, *so* pretty, *so* smart, *so* nice. I think a lot of the girls felt, well, threatened by you. So we took Kathleen."

Corinne was smiling at me now. She seemed calm, almost happy. Her face didn't quite match the words she was saying.

What was going on? I mean, I appreciated

the truth, but why was she telling me this? Why Corinne?

"Thanks," I said, for lack of anything else to say.

Corinne returned to her group. I began walking to the gym door.

The gym was empty except for the cheerleaders. The other girls were long gone. I kept my eyes on the floor as I left. Corinne's face kept coming back to me. That smile . . .

Suddenly it was as clear as day. She was *enjoying* telling me the truth. She knew it would hurt. She thought I'd stolen Robert from her, and she wanted to teach me a lesson — that I should never try to be better than she was.

I marched straight to the cafeteria. I didn't even look at the BSC table. In the back, the basketball team was eating alone at The Group table.

Marty saw me first. He nudged Robert. They all looked up expectantly. Robert's eyes locked into mine.

"Did you . . . ?" he asked, his voice trailing off.

Hot tears sprung into my eyes. "No," I said. "They rejected me."

"Whaaaat?" Robert bolted up from the table. He took me by the arm and brought me to a

133

quiet corner. There I told him everything — Corinne's and Penny's comments, the conversation in the bathroom, the works.

By the end of my story, Robert was fuming. "Stacey, this is so unfair."

"I should have listened to you when you warned me about them," I said.

"I mean, I knew they were *vain*, but I didn't think even *they* could do something like this."

"I guess I was spoiled by you," I barged on. "I figured if someone as nice as you was in that group, they couldn't be too bad."

Robert's face fell. I realized I had said something totally stupid.

"I'm not blaming you, Robert!"

"No, no, don't worry about that," Robert replied. "You're right, though, Stacey. I mean, I do kind of turn my back on all the stuff they do."

"No, you don't. You talk about it to me, you tried to talk to Marty that morning — "

"But that's all I do, *talk*. That doesn't change anything." He took a deep breath and grabbed my hand. "Come on, Stacey."

Before I could say a word, Robert and I were jogging out of the cafeteria and down the hall to the gym. I was worried he'd burst in on the cheerleaders. I didn't want that. I never wanted to see those girls again.

But Robert detoured into a small office just before the gym. The basketball coach, Mr. Halvorsen, was sitting at his desk inside. He was reading a newspaper with his feet propped up on the desk, next to a half-eaten sandwich and an empty coffee cup.

"Heyyy, Brewster, what can I do for you?" Coach Halvorsen asked.

Robert stared him straight in the eye. "Coach, I quit."

I don't know who was more surprised, the coach or me. Both of our jaws dropped open.

"Uh, say *what*?" Coach Halvorsen said. "I don't think I'm hearing you right."

"I said I quit," Robert repeated. "As a protest. The cheerleaders led an unfair tryout."

"Cheerleaders?" the coach bellowed. "What does that have to do with us?" He gave me an accusing look.

"A lot, Coach. We're all part of the same problem. I've been thinking about this a long time. The members of the sports teams in the school — and the cheerleaders — are treated like *gods*. That kind of thing goes to people's heads. It's like, one set of rules for us, and another for everyone else. It's not fair, and I don't want to be a part of it."

The coach chuckled in disbelief. "Robert, come on. What kid doesn't want to be treated special? You guys deserve it. You're the best thing to happen to this school in twenty years."

Robert shook his head. "Maybe that's the way you feel, but I don't."

"Well, suit yourself, Robert. I've got plenty of quality players on the bench who'll be thrilled by this news."

Robert didn't answer. He and I turned and walked out the door.

CHAPTER 15

SMS NEWS & VIEWS
EDITORIAL

There is a spirit in SMS these days. It's not the school spirit we usually feel. It's not our incredible pride for the greatest sports team in recent memory, perhaps in school history. No, it's the spirit of negativity. The spirit that wants to tear us down, and for what?

Favoritism? Unfair treatment? So says a certain former mediocre player who quit the team. Well, I would like to ask him, where does he think he is? The NBA?

Maybe it was "unfair" that he missed sixty-three percent of his baskets in the last game. Maybe it was "unfair" that he had to spend part of the second half on the bench. Maybe Coach Halvorsen was showing "favoritism" to the other players, who just happened to be scoring more!

But it wasn't enough to bring down his own team. This same mediocre former player decided to bring down the cheerleaders. All because his girlfriend wasn't good enough to make the squad. "Unfair" again?

This is not the kind of spirit the rest of us feel at SMS. This is called bad attitude. And it's one thing we just don't need around here.

Nice article, huh? It came out on Wednesday, five days after Robert quit.

Lots happened over that time. Robert's quitting really shook up the school. Some kids were furious. Jason Fox refused to talk to Robert.

The good news was that *many* others approved of what Robert had done. Wherever Robert or I went, kids swamped us with questions. Apparently a lot of kids had thought the sports teams got away with murder. They'd just been too afraid to speak up.

Robert was brave. I still had the BSC, but he had a lot to lose, like his best friends. He was prepared to face angry teachers, too.

But you know what happened? The teachers and administrators called a meeting that Tuesday night to "re-evaluate the sports program." Robert and I were invited, and a committee was set up to "investigate academic abuses" and "institute a non-biased minimal grade-point standard for athletic participation." (In plain English, that means if your grades are too low, you don't play sports.)

The next day, Robert was asked to rejoin the team — first by Coach Halvorsen, then by the players themselves. To them, it was embarrassing that a star player had quit.

Robert said no.

Then, on Wednesday morning, as I was walking to homeroom, I heard someone shout, "Stacey, wait!"

It was Sheila. I had not spoken to her since the tryouts. I'd felt so betrayed by her.

"What?" I said flatly.

She looked as if she were about to cry. "Don't be mad. It wasn't my fault. I kept sticking up for you until the final vote. I know how unfair it was."

Some of my anger melted away. I believed her. "Well, thanks for telling me," I said.

"Um, Stace? I don't know if you heard — you know, about Kathleen."

"No, what?"

"Well, when she found out what had happened, she was really upset. Last night she quit."

"Really?"

"Uh-huh. So you know what that means, Stacey. That spot has opened up again. And the girls have agreed — you're the one. No tryouts necessary."

For a moment I felt a shiver of joy. But it went away quickly.

Funny. Just a few days before, I'd wanted to be on that squad so badly. Getting cut had devastated me.

Now the idea of being a cheerleader seemed silly. It was the last thing I wanted to do.

And I wondered: Why had it been so important to be friends with those girls?

I thought of Tiffany Kilbourne. She had taken a long time to realize she was trying hobbies she didn't like for all the wrong reasons.

Well, I had taken a long time, too. "No," I said gently to Sheila. "I'm doing other things."

It was true. I had my best friends, my family, my schoolwork, and baby-sitting. And I had Robert.

That was plenty for me.

* * *

Oh! I forgot to tell you about the *other* editorial that appeared in the SMS newspaper. Unlike the first one, it was signed:

> We are happy about what's been happening at SMS this week. So many students have given us their support, and we think great changes are ahead.
>
> SMS is a fantastic school. Our teachers are dedicated and our students are the best. All of us should feel we're being treated fairly. In a basketball game, every player abides by the same rules. If those rules are broken, the game stops. A timeout is called, everyone sets up, and the ball is put back in play.
>
> Well, the ball is in play again at SMS. And this time, we can all be winners.
>
> Stacey McGill and Robert Brewster

141

Dear Reader,

In *Stacey and the Cheerleaders*, Tiffany Kilbourne needs to find a hobby. As a child, I had many hobbies. I was interested in lots of things, and I was always starting new projects. I tried stamp collecting, coin collecting, macramé, and needlework. Although I was not a very active kid, I did try ballet lessons, and I took exactly three tennis lessons! I attacked each new project or hobby (except for the tennis lessons) with a vengeance, even if it didn't last long. For instance, my stamp collection began when I inherited a partially filled stamp album. I soon discovered that I could get stamps from all over the world through the mail, and I spent hours ordering and arranging stamps. For a long time one of my biggest hobbies was magic. It started when my father, an amateur magician, gave me all of his old tricks. Then, just like with the stamp collecting, I found that I could order magic tricks through the mail. I pored through catalogues, ordering new tricks. I even spent my baby-sitting money on new tricks, and then I entertained my charges with them. So the next time you're bored, just think of all the things you could try. And you can find out about most hobbies simply by going to the library. You'll be amazed by what you can find there.

Happy reading,

Ann M. Martin

L. GODWIN

Ann M. Martin

About the Author

ANN MATTHEWS MARTIN was born on August 12, 1955. She grew up in Princeton, NJ, with her parents and her younger sister, Jane.

Although Ann used to be a teacher and then an editor of children's books, she's now a full-time writer. She gets the ideas for her books from many different places. Some are based on personal experiences. Others are based on childhood memories and feelings. Many are written about contemporary problems or events.

All of Ann's characters, even the members of the Baby-sitters Club, are made up. (So is Stoneybrook.) But many of her characters are based on real people. Sometimes Ann names her characters after people she knows, other times she chooses names she likes.

In addition to the Baby-sitters Club books, Ann Martin has written many other books for children. Her favorite is *Ten Kids, No Pets* because she loves big families and she loves animals. Her favorite Baby-sitters Club book is *Kristy's Big Day*. (By the way, Kristy is her favorite baby-sitter!)

Ann M. Martin now lives in New York with her cats, Gussie and Woody. Her hobbies are reading, sewing, and needlework — especially making clothes for children.

Notebook Pages

This Baby-sitters Club book belongs to _____.

I am _____ years old and in the _____

grade.

The name of my school is _____

I got this BSC book from _____

I started reading it on _____ and

finished reading it on _____

The place where I read most of this book is _____

My favorite part was when _____.

If I could change anything in the story, it might be the part when

_____

My favorite character in the Baby-sitters Club is _____

The BSC member I am most like is _____

because _____.

If I could write a Baby-sitters Club book it would be about _____

_____

#70 Stacey and the Cheerleaders

In *Stacey and the Cheerleaders*, Stacey starts dating Robert, and even decides to try out for cheerleading. The names of the cheerleaders I know are _____ _____ · If I were a cheerleader, this is the cheer I would write for my school: _____ _____ _____ · Stacey enjoys watching the SMS boys' basketball team play. My favorite sport to watch is _____ . Unfortunately, Stacey's new friends talk behind her back. I once heard _____ talking behind my back. I felt _____ · Together, Stacey and Robert write an article for the SMS newspaper. If I were going to write an article in my school newspaper, it would be about ____ _____ _____ .

Here I am, age three.

Me with Charlott
my "almost

A family portrait — me
with my parents.

SCRAPBOOK

hanssen, ister."

Getting ready for school.

In LUV at Shadow Lake.

Read all the books
about **Stacey**
in the Baby-sitters Club series
by Ann M. Martin

THE BABY-SITTERS CLUB®

Collect 'em all!

100 (and more)
Reasons to Stay Friends Forever!

❏ MG43388-1	#1	Kristy's Great Idea	$3.50
❏ MG43387-3	#10	Logan Likes Mary Anne!	$3.99
❏ MG43717-8	#15	Little Miss Stoneybrook...and Dawn	$3.50
❏ MG43722-4	#20	Kristy and the Walking Disaster	$3.50
❏ MG43347-4	#25	Mary Anne and the Search for Tigger	$3.50
❏ MG42498-X	#30	Mary Anne and the Great Romance	$3.50
❏ MG42508-0	#35	Stacey and the Mystery of Stoneybrook	$3.50
❏ MG44082-9	#40	Claudia and the Middle School Mystery	$3.25
❏ MG43574-4	#45	Kristy and the Baby Parade	$3.50
❏ MG44969-9	#50	Dawn's Big Date	$3.50
❏ MG44968-0	#51	Stacey's Ex-Best Friend	$3.50
❏ MG44966-4	#52	Mary Anne + 2 Many Babies	$3.50
❏ MG44967-2	#53	Kristy for President	$3.25
❏ MG44965-6	#54	Mallory and the Dream Horse	$3.25
❏ MG44964-8	#55	Jessi's Gold Medal	$3.25
❏ MG45657-1	#56	Keep Out, Claudia!	$3.50
❏ MG45658-X	#57	Dawn Saves the Planet	$3.50
❏ MG45659-8	#58	Stacey's Choice	$3.50
❏ MG45660-1	#59	Mallory Hates Boys (and Gym)	$3.50
❏ MG45662-8	#60	Mary Anne's Makeover	$3.50
❏ MG45663-6	#61	Jessi and the Awful Secret	$3.50
❏ MG45664-4	#62	Kristy and the Worst Kid Ever	$3.50
❏ MG45665-2	#63	Claudia's ~~Freind~~ Friend	$3.50
❏ MG45666-0	#64	Dawn's Family Feud	$3.50
❏ MG45667-9	#65	Stacey's Big Crush	$3.50
❏ MG47004-3	#66	Maid Mary Anne	$3.50
❏ MG47005-1	#67	Dawn's Big Move	$3.50
❏ MG47006-X	#68	Jessi and the Bad Baby-sitter	$3.50
❏ MG47007-8	#69	Get Well Soon, Mallory!	$3.50
❏ MG47008-6	#70	Stacey and the Cheerleaders	$3.50
❏ MG47009-4	#71	Claudia and the Perfect Boy	$3.99
❏ MG47010-8	#72	Dawn and the We ❤ Kids Club	$3.99
❏ MG47011-6	#73	Mary Anne and Miss Priss	$3.99
❏ MG47012-4	#74	Kristy and the Copycat	$3.99
❏ MG47013-2	#75	Jessi's Horrible Prank	$3.50
❏ MG47014-0	#76	Stacey's Lie	$3.50
❏ MG48221-1	#77	Dawn and Whitney, Friends Forever	$3.99
❏ MG48222-X	#78	Claudia and Crazy Peaches	$3.50
❏ MG48223-8	#79	Mary Anne Breaks the Rules	$3.50
❏ MG48224-6	#80	Mallory Pike, #1 Fan	$3.99
❏ MG48225-4	#81	Kristy and Mr. Mom	$3.50

More titles... ➧

❏ MG48226-2	#82	Jessi and the Troublemaker	$3.99
❏ MG48235-1	#83	Stacey vs. the BSC	$3.50
❏ MG48228-9	#84	Dawn and the School Spirit War	$3.50
❏ MG48236-X	#85	Claudi Kishi, Live from WSTO	$3.50
❏ MG48227-0	#86	Mary Anne and Camp BSC	$3.50
❏ MG48237-8	#87	Stacey and the Bad Girls	$3.50
❏ MG22872-2	#88	Farewell, Dawn	$3.50
❏ MG22873-0	#89	Kristy and the Dirty Diapers	$3.50
❏ MG22874-9	#90	Welcome to the BSC, Abby	$3.99
❏ MG22875-1	#91	Claudia and the First Thanksgiving	$3.50
❏ MG22876-5	#92	Mallory's Christmas Wish	$3.50
❏ MG22877-3	#93	Mary Anne and the Memory Garden	$3.99
❏ MG22878-1	#94	Stacey McGill, Super Sitter	$3.99
❏ MG22879-X	#95	Kristy + Bart = ?	$3.99
❏ MG22880-3	#96	Abby's Lucky Thirteen	$3.99
❏ MG22881-1	#97	Claudia and the World's Cutest Baby	$3.99
❏ MG22882-X	#98	Dawn and Too Many Sitters	$3.99
❏ MG69205-4	#99	Stacey's Broken Heart	$3.99
❏ MG69206-2	#100	Kristy's Worst Idea	$3.99
❏ MG69207-0	#101	Claudia Kishi, Middle School Dropout	$3.99
❏ MG69208-9	#102	Mary Anne and the Little Princess	$3.99
❏ MG69209-7	#103	Happy Holidays, Jessi	$3.99
❏ MG45575-3		Logan's Story Special Edition Readers' Request	$3.25
❏ MG47118-X		Logan Bruno, Boy Baby-sitter Special Edition Readers' Request	$3.50
❏ MG47756-0		Shannon's Story Special Edition	$3.50
❏ MG47686-6		The Baby-sitters Club Guide to Baby-sitting	$3.25
❏ MG47314-X		The Baby-sitters Club Trivia and Puzzle Fun Book	$2.50
❏ MG48400-1		BSC Portrait Collection: Claudia's Book	$3.50
❏ MG22864-1		BSC Portrait Collection: Dawn's Book	$3.50
❏ MG69181-3		BSC Portrait Collection: Kristy's Book	$3.99
❏ MG22865-X		BSC Portrait Collection: Mary Anne's Book	$3.99
❏ MG48399-4		BSC Portrait Collection: Stacey's Book	$3.50
❏ MG92713-2		The Complete Guide to The Baby-sitters Club	$4.95
❏ MG47151-1		The Baby-sitters Club Chain Letter	$14.95
❏ MG48295-5		The Baby-sitters Club Secret Santa	$14.95
❏ MG45074-3		The Baby-sitters Club Notebook	$2.50
❏ MG44783-1		The Baby-sitters Club Postcard Book	$4.95

Available wherever you buy books...or use this order form.

Scholastic Inc., P.O. Box 7502, 2931 E. McCarty Street, Jefferson City, MO 65102

Please send me the books I have checked above. I am enclosing $_____
(please add $2.00 to cover shipping and handling). Send check or money order–
no cash or C.O.D.s please.

Name_____ Birthdate_____

Address _____

City_____ State/Zip _____